# SPELLS AND BANANAS

## *Midnight Matings*

## Joyee Flynn

**EROTIC ROMANCE**
**MANLOVE**

**Siren Publishing, Inc.**
**www.SirenPublishing.com**

**A SIREN PUBLISHING BOOK**
IMPRINT: Erotic Romance ManLove

SPELLS AND BANANAS
Copyright © 2011 by Joyee Flynn

ISBN-10: 1-61926-084-0
ISBN-13: 978-1-61926-084-9

First Printing: October 2011

Cover design by Jinger Heaston
All cover art and logo copyright © 2011 by Siren Publishing, Inc.

**ALL RIGHTS RESERVED:** This literary work may not be reproduced or transmitted in any form or by any means, including electronic or photographic reproduction, in whole or in part, without express written permission.

All characters and events in this book are fictitious. Any resemblance to actual persons living or dead is strictly coincidental.

Printed in the U.S.A.

**PUBLISHER**
Siren Publishing, Inc.
www.SirenPublishing.com

# DEDICATION

To my wonderful intern: You're doing an amazing job. I know it's challenging and I'm not easy on you, but I promise there's a method to my madness and in the end any publisher would be lucky to have you. Whether you stay the course to become a fabulous editor or decide to write yourself one day it's the most rewarding career I've ever had. This is the first book you've worked on start to finish that's coming out and you were a big part of it. Be proud of that because I'm proud of you.

# SPELLS AND BANANAS

## *Midnight Matings*

### JOYEE FLYNN
### Copyright © 2011

## Chapter 1

"And just in case you think to try and break this spell," Elder Burke said, "we have added a special clause. Anyone that attempts to negate the covenants of this spell will instantly be cursed as befitting their race. Vampires will no longer be able to drink blood. Shifters will no longer be able to shift. Magic users will have no magic, and so on. I'm sure you get my point."

The two Elders went to stand back with their fellow Elders and turned back to face the crowd. "Now, children, good luck. We expect to see each of you in twenty-four hours. May your hunt be successful."

I stood there for a split second in shock before the room detonated like an atom bomb. Then I did the only thing an intelligent person does when given a spiked drink…I stuck my finger down my throat and tried to vomit it back up. As I was ungraciously gagging, some chick groped my dick.

"Mmm, nice package. I'll take you." She purred and used her other hand to grab my shoulder. "I've always wanted monkey sex with a real monkey."

"Fuck off, cunt," I snarled, turning only my head to face her. And then she bitch slapped me. I shook it off and narrowed my eyes. "I don't have a problem hitting women."

"You shouldn't mess with me, monkey," she sneered. "I have powers beyond your comprehension."

"But not as many as I have, Meghan," a deep voice said, sending shivers down my spine.

"Amery," she gasped. "Have you called this one? I did not know."

"No, but you will unhand him immediately," he answered. In a flash her hands were gone. "I suggest you go *ask* someone else if they'd like to be your mate. You know full well our laws prevent forced mating."

While they were talking, I went back to trying to toss my cookies. The next thing I knew, she was gone and a large hand was gently stroking my back. What had she said his name was again? I swear when she smacked me she rattled my brain around.

"The spell will prevent you from banishing it from your body, little one."

"It was worth a shot." I sighed and turned around to face him. My body did a full shudder of lust at the gorgeous sight before me. "Any chance you wanted to claim me then? I mean, we have to mate, and you're hot, and you're sweet enough to have just saved me, and I am a monkey, so the sex with my kind is really hot and—"

"You're adorable when you ramble." He chuckled and cupped my cheek. "Would you really want me?"

I eyed over the reason for my hard-on like a thirsty man. He had black hair and caramel-brown eyes like I did, but his hair was just a tad longer than my short cut. But we definitely weren't built the same. I was five-five and lithe while he was probably six-five and so ripped his muscles had muscles. Though not in that obnoxious way that just screamed steroids.

"Yes please," I whimpered and dug my fingers into the wall behind me to keep from reaching out to him. "You're not a monkey, right? We have to cross mate."

"I'm a witch, and I would be honored to mate you," he said, his voice going an octave lower as his eyes filled with the same need I was feeling. "What's your name? I need to know what I'll be shouting during our hot monkey sex."

"Kirby," I moaned, giving in and reaching for him. "Kirby Saxon, but you can call me yours."

"I intend to," he purred in my ear as he leaned down and wrapped his arms around me. "All I need to know is that if we mate, there will never be another for you. I don't believe in open matings."

"I'd never cheat on my mate." Cheating on your mate was a death sentence if caught amongst monkeys, but he was talking about it as if he was expecting me to step out on him.

"Good. Some witches believe that mating doesn't mean you stop having sex with other people, but that's not what I think."

Light bulb!

"I'm so glad," I whispered into his massive chest. Then I let out a sigh. I'd never felt so safe and wanted as I did right in that moment from a simple hug from…I still didn't remember his name. "What's your name?"

"My apologies, Kirby." He chuckled. "It seems I'm only thinking with my dick right now. I'm Amery Goddard."

I leaned back in the embrace, so I could get a good look at him again and then nodded. "It suits you. I like it."

"I'm so glad," Amery said with a smirk, tossing my early words at me playfully.

We both turned when the door the Elders had left through opened again and they re-emerged.

"Do we need more time to talk, or should we be first in line and get the hell out of here?"

"We're going to have to work some things out, Kirby," he answered slowly as his eyes searched my face. "I mean, this is forever once we do this. We don't know anything about each other or—"

"I've never been so drawn, felt so safe, or gotten an insta-hard-on from someone else before," I said firmly, interrupting him. "I trust my gut, and while I'd love to take the time before officially mating to get to know everything about you, we only have twenty-four hours."

"You're right," he sighed as he nodded. "I'm just scared. You know what I mean?"

"Yeah, it's a huge step to take in the matter of a few moments. I get it. But it feels right, too. Or is that just me?" I started to pull away, realizing he might not be feeling the sparks and peace I was feeling at the idea of being mated to him.

"No, it's not just you." He pulled me back into his arms, squeezed me gently as he kissed my neck, and then stepped away. He gave me a soft smile as he took my hand and led me up to the stage. It looked out of place in a Scottish castle's ballroom because it reminded me more of the stage in the theater of my high school. I mean, it was complete with curtains and spotlights.

Were the Elders acting out plays in their spare time? The thought of some of them performing a musical was enough to make me almost burst out laughing in the midst of all the chaos. Whether they were or not, someone needed a lesson in decorating because the puke-green drapes that hid the doors on either side tied back with purple rope had to go.

I went to jump up the three feet onto it, but strong hands wrapped around my little waist and lifted me up.

"What a gentleman," I purred and gave him a wink. "I reward such manners accordingly, my big, soon-to-be mate."

"Oh really?" He swallowed loudly, and I saw his Adam's apple bob as his eyes glazed over with lust. Just the reaction I was looking for. Sweet.

"Really." I chuckled and then turned to the Elders that were standing there looking bored. "Kirby Saxon takes Amery Goddard as his mate."

"Amery, do you take this *man* as your mate?" an Elder I didn't know said with a sneer. It seemed the douche knew Amery though.

"I do, Elder Flores," Amery answered with an edge to his voice as if challenging the Elder to say something about it.

"As you wish," Elder Flores sighed, shaking his head in disgust. Yeah, this guy wouldn't be getting on my Christmas card list anytime soon. Another Elder started writing in a massive book—the *Book of Matings*. I'd never seen it before, but it lived up to its reputation. As soon as he finished, I felt white-hot pain shoot through my left shoulder blade.

Amery gasped, and I turned to him, seeing he was grabbing his right wrist. Guess that's where his mating mark would be. The pain only lasted a minute and then tingled as my shifter body went to work on healing the perceived injury.

"Ready for some monkey mating sex?" I asked my mate after we were done.

"You need this, Amery," Elder Flores said as we turned to leave, my mate practically drooling after my words. Amery grabbed the sealed envelope, which probably held another list of rules and hoops we had to jump through, and gave a respectful nod to the Elders as he stuffed it in his pocket.

"Maybe everyone won't be as pissed off as we thought," one of the Elders whispered as we walked to the edge of the stage. "I mean, the first people to sign in were more focused on each other than kicking our asses for what we did."

"Amery's a pacifist, and the boy is a monkey," Elder Flores snickered. "Don't for a second think they'll be the normal reaction we get."

"You still deserve the ass kicking," I said over my shoulder before hopping off the stage and turning to face them. "You just drugged, albeit with magic, hundreds of people. And you forced them to basically get married or they die. I'm pretty sure when the human governments are told of this little stunt you'll all be facing serious jail time."

"For the gods, why?" one Elder gasped as they all stared at me as if I was growing another head.

"Let me think," I said sarcastically before ticking off fingers. "Drugging everyone, attempted murder if they refuse your little ploy, and I'm sure someone could argue for a form of rape since you're forcing sex with a partner maybe not of their choice. Shall I go on?"

"Get him out of here, Amery," Elder Flores snarled. I turned to my mate, and we stared at each other for a moment. I held my breath as I knew this would be a defining moment in our relationship... would he back me or align with the Elders?

"How old are you, Kirby?" he asked me as he tilted his head as he studied me.

"Thirty, why?"

"Then I believe my mate is more than capable of speaking his mind without being treated as a child, Elder Flores," Amery said firmly to the douche as he smiled at me. "And I think he brings up valid points. Since you all felt the need to take away the free will of my new mate, that's seen as a transgression that allows me retribution. Does it not?"

"Be very careful, witch," another Elder hedged. "It's not wise to piss off UPAC."

"And it's not wise to piss me off or fuck with my mate," he said in a cold voice with such venom I felt myself take a step back. Holy shit! My mate could be very scary. Amery muttered something under his breath as he looked at each Elder on the stage right then in turn. "I think that's a lateral punishment for what you did."

"Son of a bitch!" one Elder cried out and jumped to his feet. I glanced between my mate and the man, waiting to be filled in on what was going on. "Seriously, witch? Hemorrhoids? What are you, twelve?"

"No, I'm a few millennia old, and you might want to remember how strong some of us are before pulling another stunt like you did tonight. I'm not going to file formal charges with the human authorities since I choose to look at what you've done as a mean-spirited prank. *However*, one mean prank deserves another. So enjoy your hemorrhoids, gents!"

"How long will we have them?" Elder Flores snarled. Oh, wasn't that interesting? Now why couldn't the Elder of the witches undo my mate's spell? I'd have to ask later, along with giving him a blow job for backing me and his ingenious retaliation. I mean, yeah, hemorrhoids were pretty damn funny. It wasn't something they could take as a serious threat, but it had to piss them off.

"Until I deem I'm no longer upset with you." Amery chuckled and took my hand as he glanced at me. "What do you think, my mate? How about until we fall in love? If we are able to make this mating work and end up better off because of it, I say we let them off the hook."

"I don't think I'll have any problem falling for you," I said softly as I stared at him with awe. How fucking cool was my mate? Damn, I might end up sending the Elders a fruit basket for drugging us after all.

"Still, I think they should suffer a bit."

"Agreed. Now let's get out of here and forget them and their hemorrhoids," I said and squeezed his hand in mine. Amery nodded with a smile and a growing bulge behind his dress pants. Seems I wasn't the only one excited about what came next. "Oh and I will be writing an article about this. Have fun dealing with the fallout of that, gents!"

"What does the monkey do?" one Elder asked as Amery spoke at the same time.

"What is your profession, Kirby?"

"I'm a columnist and reporter for *Sups Weekly*," I answered with pride. I loved my job. *Sups Weekly* was like *TIME Magazine* and *People* rolled into one without all the gossip of who's sleeping with whom. This was news about our world and stories of paranormals in charge and trying to swim in the human world. "How about you?"

"I'm Chief Nursing Officer at Colorado Springs Hospital," he answered with a blush.

"Now why would you be embarrassed with that?" I asked as I ducked as some shifter dove at me, or at something behind me. Who knew what was going on in this chaos? "I think that's an honorable profession."

"Most people look down on male nurses," Amery said quietly before shoving past two vamps and another shifter. Damn, that shifter did *not* look happy as he stormed to the stage. I had a feeling the Elders were about to get their first majorly unhappy customer.

We exited the ballroom as I thought about what he said, mulling it over. He took my silence the wrong way and started rambling as he led me to the magical wing of the castle.

"I have enough training to be a doctor. I was a medicine man for several centuries, but in the current health care structure, I felt that nurses are the heart of the medical profession. I get to interact with patients more often now and use my years of experience to help the new nurses and—"

"Amery, stop," I said gently, interrupting him. I pulled on his arm so he had to face me. "I was thinking about how logical what you said was. I wasn't judging you in any way. You're much older than me, and you have *centuries* of experience that I don't. If you want to be a nurse, and it makes you happy, then no one has the right to look down on that, and I never would."

"I'm glad I saw what Meghan was trying to do to you," he whispered. "Otherwise we might not have met, and I'd be stuck mated to someone else who possibly would not get me as you already clearly do."

"I'm glad, too," I purred, standing on my toes. He got the idea and reached out with his free hand, cupping the back of my head and neck as he leaned down. Amery's lips brushed mine hesitantly as we got a feel for each other. Once. Then twice before moving back enough for us to see into each other's eyes. I saw his were sparkling with lust as I started breathing heavily.

The sparks I felt in those two quick kisses were more than I had in my life. I stared at the lips I wanted to feel on mine and my body often. As I did, Amery licked them, and I groaned at the sensual sight. His mouth was so much softer than I would have thought. Did he use ChapStick or something?

If he did, I'd get him bags full of it if it kept his lips so inviting.

"Good?" he asked hoarsely. I nodded, unable to put what I felt into words. "More?"

"Oh yeah," I whimpered seconds before he mashed his mouth down to mine. I moaned and instantly opened for him. Amery gently slid his tongue over mine, exploring every inch of my mouth. He coaxed my tongue back into his mouth, and I didn't hesitate. It could have been minutes or hours that we stood there kissing, ignoring the world around us.

That was until someone crashed into us.

"Let's continue this in my room." He panted as we broke apart. I smiled brightly at him and let go of the death grip I'd had on his biceps.

I wanted to purr something silly like, "my, what big arms you have." But I was able to bite my tongue for once and hurried along with him as he led the way.

"Where do you live, sweets?" Amery asked as he opened a solid oak door for me that looked like it could withstand a bomb. I assumed it led to the magical wing. It was also really, really big. Were there even giants? Who used these doors?

The torches all over the castle and hallways cast creepy shadows that might have freaked me out if I didn't have Amery at my side. But the stone work and architecture was amazing.

"Orlando, but I can live anywhere with my job."

"So you'd be cool with moving in with me? Could you like Colorado Springs?" We rushed up the stairs as we talked. It warmed my heart that he seemed as excited to get naked as I was.

"I'd love to live with you," I answered, being completely honest. I'd follow this massive, hot, sweet-hearted man anywhere, I had a feeling. "You're not like up, way up in the mountains or anything? I mean, it's like a real city, right?"

"Yes, we have just about everything." He chuckled. Amery waved his hand, and I heard the lock disengage before the door opened.

"Oh you're handy to have around! I bet our life will never be boring."

"I hope not," Amery growled softly. He kicked the door closed after we entered his room and pushed me back against it. I let out a shocked yelp, and then his lips were back on mine. Mmm good. We kissed, licked, sucked, and nipped on each other's mouths like starving men. And on a scale of one to ten, the passion had to be at least a twenty. Nice.

"More," I moaned and tried to crawl up his body. He stood up enough for me to do it, moving his hands under my ass, and lifted. I wrapped my legs around his hips as I started to unbutton his shirt. He wore a gorgeous silk shirt the same color as his eyes, and I liked it a lot. Otherwise I wouldn't have cared and shredded it. "Skin."

"Guess we're not going to have any issues in the bedroom department." I saw the mirth shining in his eyes right before he pulled my shirt up. I smiled at him and raised my arms overhead to help him. Once it was off, I went back and undid the last two buttons. I took my time sliding the material off his wide, muscular shoulders, drinking in every inch of his skin.

"No, no, I don't think we'll have any problems there," I whispered in awe of his body. Hot damn! I couldn't have come up with a hotter man in my fantasies, and he found me. I was a lucky, lucky little monkey. "And if I'm ever not in the mood, just feed me a banana."

"Seriously?" He laughed as he walked us over to the bed. "How about chocolate-covered ones?"

"Gods, you're the perfect man for me," I moaned. I loved chocolate-covered fruit, especially bananas. "Yeah, it's like giving a monkey Viagra."

"Good to know," Amery said against my lips as he laid me back on the bed. "I have a confession. Something I've never told anyone before, but you're my mate, and I want to always be honest with you."

"Okay," I whispered, scared that my mate was about to tell me he was Jack the Ripper or something.

"I like to bottom," he blurted out and then started rambling. "I know with my size everyone assumes I'm a top. And don't get me wrong, I love the feeling of thrusting into a warm body but—"

"This is the *only* body you'll be thrusting into or ever touching again," I said with a snarl. "Am I crystal fucking clear?"

"Of course," he moaned. "It's hot when you get all riled up and dominant."

"Good, then get your clothes off *now* and find some lube," I replied forcefully. I was an easygoing guy most times, but if it got my mate hot for me to take charge in bed sometimes, I was pretty sure I could suffer through that. Yeah, it would be a real hardship.

"Yes, my mate." Amery shivered as he hopped off the bed and started yanking off clothes.

"Yeah, you have to promise to still top me sometimes." I just about swallowed my tongue as he let loose his third leg of an erection, salivating at the idea of that pounding into my ass. "I want to feel your monster cock in me sometimes."

"Of course," he said with a wide smile as he purposely bent over and gave me an exquisite view of his very round, muscular globes as he reached into his suitcase.

The second I saw his pink star winking at me, I moved faster than I ever thought possible. By the time he turned back around I was completely naked and pushing my clothes off the bed. His eyes went wide as he zeroed in on my groin.

"I'm not the only one with a third leg." Amery glanced up from my cock to my face and back down as he licked his lips.

"What? This little thing?" I teased as I spread my legs wide and stroked my leaking prick. I was pretty short but blessed between the legs. I had seven inches, which I knew to be rare for someone five-five. But what kept my previous partners as happy as Amery looked was my girth. I couldn't even close my hand around my cock it was so big. "You like?"

"Yes," he growled as he tossed the lube by my hip. In a flash he was on his knees between my spread knees hanging off the edge of the bed. "I need to know I can swallow you."

That was the only warning I got before he grabbed my dick and sucked the head into his mouth. I cried out at the sudden pleasure as I leaned back on my hands. There was no way I was missing this show. Amery's eyes never left mine as he licked and sucked just under the head, his mouth stretched wide around me. It was the most erotic sight ever.

"Swing up here," I panted, and he gave me a confused look. "I need to get you ready, and if you keep that up, I'm going to blow soon."

He deep-throated me once, his lips touching my skin. Guess that answered that question! And then he pulled off with a slurp.

"I already stretched myself for you magically."

"Okay, I get that, but next time I do it myself," I said with a pout. I knew we were both on edge, but I liked stretching out my partner. It was silly even though I couldn't help how I felt. It just seemed wrong that he prepared himself without even asking me or considering what I wanted for our first time together. But maybe he just didn't have enough blood in his brain to think of that?

I wasn't sure, but my doubt and slight hurt had my cock deflating. Amery noticed as I quickly moved my hands to my lap. I didn't want something so small to put a damper on our first time together. He glanced up at me, and I saw the hurt look in his eyes as he started to pull away. Well shit, this wasn't what I was picturing for our mating sex. Fuck!

# Chapter 2

"I'm sorry, I wasn't thinking," Amery whispered as he sat back on his heels and ran his hands up my thighs.

"No, it's okay. I'm just being silly," I quickly said and stared at his chest. He slipped his fingers under my chin as he leaned back in and lifted my face, so I had to meet his gaze.

"Anything you ever feel isn't silly, Kirby. Don't ever think that with me. I want to know if I'm an idiot or hurt your feelings. And I'm sorry. I should have asked or said something before I did it. I was just so excited for you to claim me that I knew it would make things go faster. That and I know we both want to get out of here and to our home. Will you forgive me?"

"Yes, of course," I whispered and leaned in to kiss him.

My heart warmed at his words and pushed out all the doubts in my mind. I could fully understand getting so excited that he was thinking with the wrong head. And yes, we did want to get out of the castle before they threw something else at us, so his reasoning was sound.

"It is a neat trick that you can get yourself ready like that. But the first time we make love in our bed when we get to your house, I want to prepare you myself. I want to take care of you, take the time to stretch you."

"I'd like that," Amery said as he crawled up on the bed next to me.

There was that awkward moment that everyone has with a new lover…where we stared at each other wondering what came next. Should I make a move? Let him make the move? Maybe stop being so eager and play a little coy?

I mentally smacked myself across the face. This wasn't just any lover. It was my mate, and I wouldn't start eternity together playing games.

"Thank the gods," he whimpered as I rolled onto him and started kissing his massive chest. "At work, I know what to do, always. But the rest of the time I admit I'm a little awkward and never seem to know what I should be doing."

"No games between us, Amery." I licked his right nipple to keep my words light. "I was just wondering if I shouldn't show how much I wanted this—be too eager. But I don't want that for us."

"Agreed," he moaned as I latched onto his other nipple and sucked hard. "I want us to always be comfortable around each other and honest."

"Deal," I said firmly and shimmied down his body. I knelt between his legs and stared at his hard cock for a moment. "Well, hello there. I'm Kirby, and you and I are going to be great, great friends."

Amery started to chuckle until I swallowed him down. Holy shit! I only had about half of his dick in my mouth before it hit the back of my throat. Well, practice makes perfect!

"Please, Kirby, I need you in me."

"As my mate wishes," I purred after I pulled off his cock with a pop. "Can you claim me in this position? How does it work for witches?"

"Yes, it's a binding incantation I'll say before we come."

"Sweet." I lifted his legs, pushing his knees to his chest as I lined up my cock with his hole.

"Condom?"

I glanced up at his face for a moment, completely confused. "We're good without one."

"Really?" he gasped his face lighting up like the Fourth of July.

Umm, okay? Was Amery so used to being with humans that he'd never gone bareback before? It was common knowledge that shifters couldn't get or give human diseases, and shifter illness were very rare and never sexually transmitted. I'd have to ask about that later, but right now I didn't want the real world interfering with our mating sex.

"Really," I moaned as I pushed inside of him. Damn, that spell rocked! He was perfectly slicked and stretched out for me. I watched where our bodies connected in awe. His tight hole stretching to accommodate me as if his body wanted me there as much as I did.

Amery wrapped his legs around my hips when I bottomed out inside of him. It was the most heavenly, magical feeling I'd ever had…and not just because he was a witch. It was Amery. This was right, and I knew no matter how we got there, we were meant to be mates.

"You feel it, too?" he whispered, almost as if he didn't want to break the trance we were in. I nodded as I leaned forward, folding him in half so I could move my hands under his shoulders.

"It's like coming home to a place I never knew I was missing," I said softly as I stared into his sparkling caramel eyes.

"Yes. As if my whole life was leading up to me finding you to start really living."

"But that's crazy, right?" I asked, more to myself than him, but when I saw Amery's face fall with disappointment, I wished I could kick my own ass right then. "I feel it, too, Amery. Don't doubt that, okay?"

"Okay," he said with a nod, though his eyes didn't revert to their previous bliss, and I wanted to change that.

"I only meant that I'd never heard that mating could be like this in a world where there are not fated mates like you read in books." I started moving my hips slowly because if I didn't, I thought I was going to lose my mind. Amery was perfect, his body and the way he felt better than any dream I could ever have had. The temptation to take him was just too much to resist.

Not that he was complaining of course, but I probably should have waited until we were done talking. He just seemed so sad, and it might have been a cheap shot to take him when he was obviously distracted. I just wanted us to focus on us, nothing else.

"I thought you were saying that I'm crazy," he admitted and turned his head away from me.

"Wait—what? No! Amery, no!" I stuttered and gasped. "Don't ever think that! I just meant the intense feelings we're having after the mating seals seem a little nutty to me. But if you're crazy, I'm right there with you, babe."

I almost fell on top of him ungracefully as I moved both hands at once to turn his face back to me. I was able to right myself at the last moment with my left hand while my right hand grabbed his chin. Growling when he fought me, I turned his face to me none too gently.

"No games and no hiding, remember?" I snarled as I moved so our noses were touching. Then I switched tactics when I saw him practically crawl into himself as his face seemed to shut down on me when his eyes lost focus and expression went blank. I kissed the tip of his nose and then each of his eyes. "Why do I think this is more than just you thinking I called you crazy, my mate?"

"You're right. I'm sorry," he said sheepishly as if the light bulb went off over his head, and he just put the pieces together. "I'll tell you everything but later, if that's okay?"

His smile was so hesitant, almost frightened, that I knew I wasn't going to like this. But I pushed my feeling to the side. Amery needed me, needed to be loved more than anything if his actions since we'd met were any indication. And I was just the man for the job.

"Nothing else right now but us," I whispered against his lips and thrust into him hard. "Us and mating sex. Everything else waits at the door and takes a number for when we're done."

"Right. Right, sounds good," Amery moaned as he lifted his hips to meet me. "Just us, only our mating."

"Your compliance is appreciated." I winked at him and quickly kissed him when I saw he was going to start laughing as the corners of his mouth crinkled. And then we got to the hot monkey sex.

I intertwined our fingers and moved them over his head as I snapped my hips faster.

"Oh gods, yes, like that," Amery exclaimed as he went wild beneath me. "Do you bite me?"

"No," I grunted, not slowing down our rhythm. "I'll shift and throw feces on you."

"What!" he gasped as he tried to get out from underneath me.

"Kidding!" I laughed and then changed angles to nail his sweet spot. "I'll shift, my monkey will sniff your neck, and then I will beat my chest in approval. That's it."

"Smart-ass," he mumbled as he raised his head and then took my lips in a toe-curling kiss.

When we both needed air, we broke apart and simply stared at each other. I made sure my flat stomach was grinding against his leaking cock as I fucked him with everything I had.

"Perfect and no condom," he moaned. What was with him and the lack of condom? Before I could process what he'd said, Amery started whispering in a language I didn't recognize. All I could tell was it was very old. Then he switched back to English. "Do you accept me as yours, Kirby Saxon?"

"I do, Amery Goddard," I said softly. Suddenly I needed to come right then or I thought my heart would stop. With energy I didn't know I had, I pounded into my mate. I just needed to hang on until…Amery cried out as he filled the space between us with his release. Now that he found his climax, I let go to have my own. "Amery!"

My orgasm hit me like a two-by-four upside the head. I screamed as I shot deep inside of him with one more thrust. Our bodies shook with the force of our releases. It seemed like hours that we came even though rationally I knew it was minutes, but his gaze never left mine.

"Gotta do it now," I whispered as I pulled out of him and he lowered his legs. Amery nodded as he gasped for air, his chest heaving. I crawled from between his legs to the side of his body, still kneeling, and shifted.

"Oh, you're so cute," he cooed and reached out to touch my fur. I was a tiny monkey, a spider monkey to be exact.

I pushed past his hand, put mine on his shoulder, and leaned over to sniff his neck. Yeah, my monkey liked...a lot. Amery smelled perfect to my animal. I stood back up on the bed, jumping around as I beat my chest and yelled out. I'd found my mate! My monkey was thrilled as much as the human side of me was.

Amery gasped as I felt the same thing I had earlier. This need for my mate as if our souls were snapping into place as one.

I quickly shifted back and smacked the side of his hip. He got the idea and immediately rolled over. The animal, even a smaller animal like a monkey, in me was thrilled that our mate was submitting to us like this. Amery presented his ass, holding his cheeks apart for me as he buried his face in the pillow. I lined up my dick and slammed back into him.

Leaning over, I grabbed Amery's cock and gave it three good tugs as I pounded into him. That's all it took. He moaned and shuddered as he came all over my hand and the bedding below him. I shouted his name as his ass clamped down on me. It was like sweet torture as I pumped more of my seed into his hot hole. I yelled until my voice was hoarse, and I was completely spent.

"Holy shit," Amery gasped as I collapsed on his back. "I feel like a teenager who can't hold his load. I've never come that quickly and especially after already having one round of hot sex."

"Welcome to being mated to a monkey." I chuckled and kissed his back.

"I'm sooo not complaining," he drawled as I slid off of him and pulled out. He fell to the bed next to me, rolling over so we were facing each other. We traded a few soft kisses, basking in the sex afterglow. Then he moved the fingertips of his right hand lightly over my face. "I'm glad your monkey likes me."

"He *really* likes you as much as I do," I admitted as I felt my cheeks heat up.

"I kinda figured that out when you were willing to make a baby with me," Amery said with a chuckle.

"Baby?" I scrunched my eyebrows together in confusion as I stared at him as if waiting for the punch line. "Who's making a baby?"

"Kirby, no," he cried out as his face fell, his eyes going wide as they filled with tears. Then he leapt out of bed and raced to the adjoining bathroom. I was up in a flash and following him.

"Amery?" I whispered in fear as I skidded to a stop. He'd already had the faucet turned on and taken down the handheld showerhead. I watched as he bent over and started washing my cum out of him. "Amery, you're scaring me."

"You didn't know. I thought you knew. I swear I did," he rambled as tears leaked from his eyes. Well, I was pretty sure that's what it was and not just the water. "I thought you wanted a baby. I was thrilled you didn't want to wear a condom already in our mating. It's fast, but with what we felt, I thought you wanted everything with me. I'm so stupid. So fucking stupid."

"*Amery!*" I finally just screamed. That got his attention. He glanced at me then, his eyes darting all around the bathroom and not focusing on me.

"You didn't know witches and all magics can get pregnant, right?"

"Th–The c–condom," I gasped, the pieces starting to fall into place. "The *men* can get pregnant?"

"Yes, our power allows our bodies to adapt and make a womb for a baby with our mates," he answered, hanging his head in shame as he started cleaning his hole again. "I thought you wanted us to have a baby. I thought you wanted to make a baby with me. I don't really think this will work in stopping it, but if it's not something you want then—"

I didn't hear the rest of what he said as the world went dark and I fainted. Hell, I didn't even have time to worry about where my body would fall. I'd probably end up cracking my head open on the tile.

Damn.

\* \* \* \*

I knew I was still out and dreaming, but I went with it and decided to use the time to think how the *fuck* I'd apologize to my mate. Not only had I pissed all over his happiness and excitement about making a baby, albeit not on purpose. I'd passed out when I found out. It would take a miracle for him not to kick me to the curb after pulling that shit!

But why did I faint? I mean, I knew it was shock, of course. Over what though? That we might have just made a baby? That I could be a dad in nine months? Assuming it was nine months gestation like a human. Or was it just that there were men that could *have* babies and my mate was one of them?

The more I thought about it, I was pretty sure it was that last one. How was Amery getting pregnant even possible?

In my dream we were in the hospital, and Amery was about to deliver. And I was excited. We could have a little girl with curly black hair and caramel eyes! Or a baby boy who would grow up big and strong like Amery. Maybe he or she would be a monkey shifter like me. But the main point I was focused on was that it felt right. Having a baby with Amery.

I wanted that. I'd never dreamt of being a dad after I realized I was gay. It just never seemed like an option. Now it was though, and I realized my heart and head were saying the same thing. A baby with Amery would be a blessing I embraced.

Yes, there would be logistics to work out, and it wasn't something I wanted immediately. It made sense to spend some time with just me and Amery, but even if he was pregnant right now, we had nine months to get ready. And I worked from home, so it wasn't like one of us would have to take a maternity leave. Though maybe a part-time nanny would work, too.

The more I thought about it, us having a small bundle of joy, the more excited I got. And that must have woken me up because as Amery started to push in my dream, and as I was about to find out if it was a boy or a girl, I came back around.

And then I groaned. There was a splitting pain in the back of my head. Guess I used that to break my fall.

"Kirby, please wake up," Amery said softly but with a panicked edge to his voice. "I'm sorry I freaked you out, okay? Just wake up."

"Yes," I whispered as my eyes fluttered open.

"Yes, what, my mate?"

"Let's make a baby," I answered, trying to smile but gasping as the pain shot through my head and neck again. "Ouch. So I landed on my head?"

"Yes," he whispered his eyes going wide as he searched my face. "You're serious?"

"Yes." I gave him a wink and air kisses because that didn't seem to hurt. "I'm sorry I reacted like that. It was the shock. Not at the idea of having a baby with you, but that you *could* have one. Please don't be upset."

"No, Kirby, I'm not upset. I was worried you'd think I was trying to trick you into knocking me up and then scared shitless you were hurt badly when you smashed your head. But you've already stopped bleeding, and I can feel the gash healing."

I told him about my dream as he helped me sit up and leaned me against the vanity. My mate nodded as he listened, rinsing out the washcloth and reapplying it to my head. When I was done, I could see his face had smoothed out, and the worry lines were gone.

"I'm sorry I wigged out like that and hopped in the shower. I just, yeah, I freaked."

"Nothing to be sorry for." I snickered. "I fainted. I thought you'd toss my ass to the curb for how I reacted."

"Never," Amery said firmly as he dropped the washcloth and held my face in his hands gently. "Short of cheating on me, I'm never getting rid of you. I'm in this forever, and I take that seriously. One mix-up and fainting spell won't scare me away."

"I'll never cheat, Amery," I replied softly. I could already tell this was an issue from his past that we needed to discuss. "In monkey culture it's a death offense if caught cheating on your mate. Monkeys treat mates as a gift from the gods. We don't cheat on them."

"Good," he sighed as he helped me stand. "Not about the death sentence part. That seems archaic. But the treating mates as a gift and not stepping out on them."

"Did your ex-boyfriend cheat on you?" I asked hesitantly. He was quiet as we walked back into the bedroom and got dressed. I didn't push, simply sat on the bed when I was done and watched him pull out his suitcase.

"Yes, with a woman," Amery finally said. He wouldn't look at me as he pulled clothes out of the dresser and packed them. I wasn't going to force him. He needed to get this out his own way. "He's human and was so far in the closet I'm surprised he didn't live in it. And he wanted kids…boatloads of them. I thought about telling him I was a witch and could have them, but—"

"You didn't want him to stay just for that or risk freaking him out even more when he couldn't admit he was gay," I said when he paused and didn't start talking again. Nodding as a show of support, I understood his position and sympathized.

"Yeah, pretty much," he sighed and stuffed the rest of his stuff in the suitcase. Amery zipped it up and then sat down next to me. "He ended up having a fiancée and was with her the whole time we dated. I know what he did was wrong and completely his fault, but I took it hard. I just felt so stupid that I didn't see what was right in front of me. I mean, how did I miss *that*, you know?"

"I get it." I reached over and took his hand in mine. "I'm sorry he hurt you. He didn't deserve you, Amery. But from here on out, it's just you and me. And I'm so out that I've marched in parades and have a bumper sticker saying that I'm gay. I promise you never ever have to worry about me going after women. Girly bits scare me. I mean, what are you supposed to even do with boobs?"

"You're just saying that to make me laugh." Amery chuckled.

"It worked, didn't it?"

He leaned down and brushed his lips over mine. "Thank you for that. You have no idea how much it means to me."

"I meant it, my mate. I want you happy, Amery. And if that means dispelling a few fears and issues, that's a small thing in the grand scheme of things."

"Who knew my gorgeous mate was so smart?" He gave me a sly wink as he stood.

"I did! I did!" I playfully exclaimed as I raised my hand in the air. Amery threw back his head and let out a heartwarming laugh. Oh yeah, happy looked good on my man. I knew right then I'd do just about anything to keep him this way. "Let's go home."

"I love that you immediately called my house our home." Amery purred as he grabbed my hand and pulled me up into his arms. I instinctively wrapped myself around his body and sighed into the hug. This was truly home for me. Right there in his loving arms.

And didn't that scare the holy hell out of me since we'd just met a few hours ago.

# Chapter 3

We quickly went back to my room, and Amery changed our flights as I stuffed my belongings into my two carry-on bags. He was still on the phone when I was done, and we headed toward the main entrance.

"Seals?" A beefy dude asked as he blocked the door. I blinked rapidly at him, wondering what he was talking about. Amery chuckled and showed his wrist to the man.

Ahhh, mating seals. Duh! He let us pass, gesturing for one of the other guards to come over. The new guy jogged over and introduced himself with keys in his hand, so I guessed he was our ride.

I took Amery's hand, sliding my fingers over his seal as I did. He gave a slight shiver from the contact, and I smiled at the ability to affect him like that. I planned on spending a lot of time playing with that new hot spot of my mate's. We'd not taken too much time to explore during our mating sex.

I'd fix that *real* soon.

"I don't know if I want to chuckle at how cute you are when you bat your lashes like that or jump you because it's sexy as all get-out," Amery murmured in my ear after we climbed in the back seat of the car.

"Both?" I replied sweetly and batted them just for him.

"Tease," he growled and nipped my neck.

"Who's teasing? Monkeys have no shame," I said with a purr. "You could fuck me right now in front of our driver, and I wouldn't bat an eyelash."

"Oh sweet heavens," Amery moaned and rubbed his hand over my groin. His glance darted to the guy driving. "Keep your eyes on the road."

"Yes, sir," the dude answered in a husky voice. I met his glance in the review mirror and winked.

"You're going to kill me, you little exhibitionist." Amery chuckled. And then to my surprise...unbuttoned my fly. Before I could even comment, he unzipped me, pulled out my cock, leaned over, and took me in his mouth.

"Shit!" I gasped as my eyes practically rolled back in my head. "Oh gods, Amery. Yeah, suck it, my mate."

"Fuck," the driver gasped.

"Wish you were getting head, too?" I smirked at him.

"Wish I was the one blowing you actually," he admitted as his cheeks heated up with embarrassment. "You're a hot little piece."

"Mine," Amery growled and then swallowed my cock right back down. I'm sure there was something I should have said to defuse the tension, but all the blood wasn't in my brain just then. Besides, it was really just harmless teasing, right?

It didn't take long with his expert mouth and the guy in the front seat fantasizing he was part of it. It wasn't that he was watching, because he wasn't while driving...It just kicked up the kink factor to new levels I'd never been a part of. I would have been embarrassed how quickly I came if I wasn't so focused on my enjoyment of the blow job.

"Amery!" I cried out as I shot into his hot mouth. He drank my cum down greedily, staring up at me as lights flashed behind my eyes. The car swerved a bit before the dude righted it. "Don't fucking kill us!"

"Sorry," the guy grunted. Was he jacking off while we were playing and driving? Well, that was a new one for me.

"You rock," I panted, cupping Amery's cheek as he pulled off of me. He gave me a sly smile and then licked me clean; even though I was pretty sure I was already. Who was I to complain?

Next thing I knew, Amery was tucking me back into my jeans and the car was pulling over. I felt a goofy grin spread over my face as my mate helped me out and retrieved our bags. I leaned against the car, feeling completely boneless.

"You going to make it?" Amery asked with a knowing smirk as he took my hand.

"Best blow job ever," I cooed as I moved his arm over my shoulder so I could be closer to him.

"Seriously?" He didn't look at me, seeming focused on the ticket counters as we walked through the automatic doors. "Because of me or the driver watching?"

"Don't," I whispered and pulled away. Amery stopped walking and turned to face me. "Don't do that, Amery."

"Do what?"

I searched his face for a moment and saw that he was trying to school his features. He was doing a pretty good job, but I could still see the slight anger and hurt.

"I didn't ask for you to do that in front of the driver," I said quietly and stared at my feet, my eyes starting to burn. "It didn't matter to me if he was there or not. I don't get off on being an exhibitionist or something. In monkey culture it's just not an issue if others are around. It doesn't faze me. That's different than getting off on others watching. But you just assume I'm like your cheating ex and need more than you can give me. That's not fair."

It might have been a cheap shot, but it had truth to it. This wasn't about me. It was his issues. As he stood there stunned at what I said, I grabbed my bags from him and went over to the ticket counter. I was pissed, and maybe it wasn't the most adult thing to do, but I was hurt, too.

Standing in line, I felt numb. That had been the best blow job ever, and Amery ruined it with his issues. And I got that he had a past and problems. Hell, he was a couple millennia old. It was to be expected. But when he put them on me like that, it wasn't cool or something I'd keep taking blame for. I wasn't going to be punished for his past.

"May I help you?" the lady at the ticket counter said, snapping me out of my thoughts. I quickly glanced up and saw the line had moved forward.

"Right, sorry," I said sheepishly as I walked quickly to her station. "I have a ticket that was just changed to Colorado Springs, but I want to change it back to Orlando, please."

"You okay?" she asked gently as she took my ID.

"No, but thanks."

"Kirby, please don't," Amery begged from behind me. I turned around and saw he'd been standing three people behind me in line. "I'm sorry. Please don't go to Orlando. Come home with me. I'll do better, I promise."

"Why?"

"Why what?" he asked with scrunched eyebrows as he moved around people to cut in line.

"Why should I believe you? Why do you want me to? Why shouldn't we just go our separate ways?" I blurted out, not caring who was around us. I needed assurance right then that he could get beyond his past.

"Because I didn't realize I was even putting my shit on you like that, and I'll try to stop doing that," he said in a shaky voice before taking a deep breath. "And you mean so much to me already that the idea of you not coming with me makes it feel like I'm dying inside. I don't want us to separate. I want you. I'll come to Orlando if that's what you want."

I stood there and just stared at him. I wanted to believe him. I really did. No one was perfect, and there were going to be issues. It was just a part of life and learning to be with someone new.

"The man is begging, and I don't know about you, but I've never seen such a heart-filled plea in my life," the lady said gently. "Ever had a man plead for you to stay in public like this before?"

"No, no I haven't," I answered honestly as I gazed at Amery. I took a deep breath and made a decision. "Colorado Springs, please."

"Thank you, baby," he whispered as he took a step forward and pulled me into his arms. "I'll do better. I'll really try, I swear it to you. I didn't mean to be a jerk. I'll figure out how to let the past go. Just be patient with me."

"I can be patient, Amery," I replied, leaning my chin on his chest and looking up at him. "It's just really hard when you insinuate I'm doing something wrong when I'm not. It hurts, like you have some reason not to trust me, and I've not even fucked up yet. I'm not sure how long I can be with you when it seems you're just waiting for me to betray you. That's not fair to me."

"I know." He gave me a quick kiss since we were in public, but I felt the emotion behind it. He understood what he did wrong…Now he just needed to figure out how to stop.

"Good luck, you two," the nice lady said as she held out our boarding passes and my ID with a smile.

"Thanks," I replied as I moved away from Amery and took the tickets. "Thank you for helping me to think clearly when I couldn't."

"You're quite welcome, young lad. Now go live happily ever after with your gorgeous man."

"He is hot, isn't he?" I giggled, and she waggled her eyebrows at me. I threw back my head and really laughed at her antics while Amery checked in his suitcase.

"You sure about this?" he asked hesitantly when he was done. I glanced at the hand he held out to me for a second before taking it in mine.

"Yeah, we'll work past this." I knew we could, and now that I knew Amery *wanted* to, I was in. He'd taken the first step in solving any problem: identifying it and understanding it was there.

"We've got a half hour before our flight. You want to get some souvenirs or just go wait at the first-class lounge?"

"First class?" I asked as I looked at the boarding passes in my hand. Sure enough, my mate upgraded me to first class. Sweet!

"Nothing but the best for my mate," he whispered as he leaned down and nuzzled my neck. "I am sorry I ruined our fun in the car."

"We'll just have to do it again," I replied with a breezy air. I didn't want to focus on it or hold a grudge about it when he'd apologized and said he'd work on his issues.

"I'll give you head twice a day if you stay with me, Kirby."

"While I'm going to be a big idiot here." I chuckled and squeezed his hand. "That's not needed, Amery. You don't have to figure out ways to keep me like some contract. We're in this together. I just want you to trust me and eventually love me. The rest and the hot sex will fall into place naturally."

"What if I want to?"

"Then be my guest!"

"Now? Can I make it up to you now?" he asked as he glanced around for a secluded place.

"Let's just go shop for a bit before our flight," I answered as I saw a cute little gift shop. I loved that he was offering, but I didn't want his affections that way. I wanted him to be intimate with me when *he* wanted to, not because he thought he had to get on his knees to keep me. I didn't know what was going on in his head, but I thought it might be a lack-of-self-esteem issue. It didn't seem that Amery thought he deserved anyone to just love him for him.

It made me sad and determined to make him see himself the way I was starting to. He had a lot to give, and he was a catch.

"Whatever my mate wants," he said with a smile as we walked over to the store.

"What do you want, Amery?"

"You. All I want is you and for you to be happy with me," Amery said firmly.

"Amery," I sighed and moved under his arm so he could wrap it around my shoulder. "I want you to be happy, too, okay? We don't have to do everything that you think I want. It should be give and take."

"I know, but your face lit up when you saw this place. It was my idea to pick up some souvenirs, so it works out."

"Okay, let's go." I gave him a brighter smile than I was feeling. Yes, it was just a silly gift shop and not a big deal. I just couldn't help this nagging feeling in the back of my mind that this was part of a larger issue with him.

He dropped my hand so we could look at everything in the store. We spent the next twenty minutes simply having fun. I nearly peed myself laughing so hard when he came around one shelf with a Loch Ness Monster blow-up hat. It looked like a large balloon animal that just decided to sit on his head.

"That's hot," I said with a straight face before breaking out in peals of giggles.

"I figured since you called my cock a monster it was fitting."

"Get it," I whimpered as I got hard in my jeans instantly. Amery gave me an evil smile and took the few things in my hands before heading to the counter. I watched his firm ass as he sauntered away.

Damn, that man could tempt a priest! And he knew I wanted him and thought he was hot, but he had no clue of his real appeal. Moments later he came back to me, my T-shirt, shot glass, and postcards in a bag with his hat.

"Thank you," I said graciously when I realized the little sneak paid for my stuff. "I appreciate your gift and buying my souvenirs, but I don't want you to think you're always just going to pay."

"Of course not," he replied with a wink as he moved his hand to my lower back and guided me to our gate. Yeah, I had a feeling he planned on doing just that.

We boarded the plane, stowed my carry-on bags, and got settled in our seats. I almost felt like a kid in first class. The seats were *huge,* and I was practically swimming in mine. I decided to roll with the special treatment and accepted when the flight attendant offered me champagne.

"None for me, thanks," Amery said when she asked him. I took a slow sip and waited until she was out of ear shot.

"Why not? Don't you drink?"

"I do, but we might be…" he trailed off. Right. We might be pregnant. "Do you want to talk about it?"

"Yeah, don't you?"

"Gods yes," Amery gushed, the relief in his face apparent.

"Why didn't you tell me that?" I asked, setting down my drink and pulling his hands into my lap. I closed my hands as best as I could around his massive paws. "We need to be able to talk about important stuff, Amery."

"I would have, sweetie," he said gently as he leaned in so our foreheads were touching. "But we only met like six hours ago, and we've been a little busy. I know you said you wanted to have a baby, and that made me feel so much better. But when we were in the shop, I realized I didn't know if you were ready to have a baby *now.*"

"Fate had us both at the UPAC conference," I replied gently but firmly and leaned back so he could see how serious I was. I'd had time to think about this when I'd passed out and was dreaming. "Fate also had you right there to save me from that chick when we met. We clicked. If fate decides that you're going to get pregnant from our mating sex, then I'm going to trust fate."

"That simple?" he asked with a wary look.

"I would have liked to move into kids a little slower and wait until we were in love, but if it's now, I'm not against that, and we'll figure it out. I mean, even if you are pregnant, we have nine months to get ready for the baby."

"Three months. It's shorter because it's magic and not human growth," Amery whispered and scrunched his face in a cringe.

"Three months," I repeated then swallowed loudly. I dropped his hands for a moment, grabbed my drink, and chugged it down. Of course it went down the wrong pipe, and I started coughing.

"You okay?"

"Give me a minute to digest that," I said with a nod as I recovered. I held up my empty glass to the flight attendant. She came over with a fresh glass that was full and took mine. I set it on the tray and turned back to Amery. "I don't know anything about babies, Amery."

"So you don't want it?" His face fell in a way that broke my heart.

"No!" I gasped. "I'm not saying that. I just mean three months isn't a lot of time to learn what I need to if you're carrying our child. Do you know about kids?"

"Yes, I've worked in pediatrics for centuries," he answered, the smile back. "So you're just voicing your fears. You wouldn't want me to get an abortion or anything?"

"No, never," I replied adamantly. "If we made a child, I want him or her! This is just a lot to digest, and I need to wrap my mind around it."

"Fair enough." Amery raised my hands to his lips and kissed each one. It was maybe the most romantic gesture another man had ever given me. And didn't that just make me a sappy fool. Not that I cared. If being a sap meant I got this flutter in my stomach when he did things like that…Sign me up!

The captain came over the loudspeaker and announced we were going to taxi for take-off. I quickly downed my drink, not choking on it this time, and handed the glass back to the flight attendant when she came around.

We took off with no issues, and when we were at cruising altitude, the announcement about how long the flight was going to be came over the speakers, and the "fasten seat belt" light went off. I turned in my big seat and pulled my knees to my chest as Amery and I stared at each other for a while.

"Are you scared? Does it make me a wuss that I'm frightened to take care of another living being? I mean, we're going to be parents."

"Maybe, Kirby. We don't know for sure, and it takes more than once normally."

"True," I said slowly. His words calmed my fears a bit, but that wasn't an answer. "You ignored my questions though."

"Yes, I'm nervous, but I've had a long, long time to get used to the idea that one day I'd be a father. The idea and application are very different though. I mean, I'm freaking at the idea of popping out a baby since I'm minus a uterus and all that."

"Shit," I hissed, feeling like an ass. "I'd not even thought of that! Here I am worried about taking care of a baby, and you've got to *carry* it. Damn, I'm an idiot, and now I'm rambling and looking like a bigger jackass but—"

"Kirby, just breathe." He chuckled as he wrapped his arms around me. "You're fine. You're not a jackass, and we'll figure it all out. The part I focus on is, whether now or later, we're going to make a baby. Part you and part me, and we're going to love that baby so much."

"Do we know if it will be a witch? Or part witch and part monkey? How does that work?"

"I don't know, but does it matter?" I felt his body go stiff as stone as I leaned against him.

"Nope, not in the slightest! I'm simply trying to get as much information as possible. In my dream I pictured a precious baby girl with curly black hair and your eyes."

"We have the same color eyes, you goof." He chuckled.

"Yeah, but yours are bigger, brighter, and I think our child should definitely have your eyes."

"I'll see if we can swing that."

"Good, it's important to have a plan." I snickered and buried my face in his chest. I knew we were being sarcastic and teasing each other, but we needed to have a little fun. "I'm glad I decided on Colorado Springs."

"Me, too," Amery whispered. He nuzzled my neck and pulled me closer. I had to bite back a moan when he started placing soft kisses on my neck and shoulders. "I want you, Kirby."

"Again?" I panted, my cock liking the idea.

"I've never gotten so fucking hot from pleasing someone before. I shot in my pants when I gave you head. That's how much I enjoyed it and those little monkey noises you make. I want more. I want you always."

"Okay," I squeaked out as I quickly pulled back and hopped out of my seat. I strolled to the lavatory, giving Amery a wink over my shoulder and acting like I didn't have a raging hard-on in my jeans again. He got the idea and followed me a minute later. And yes, I got head again. Damn, he was going to spoil me rotten!

Not that I was complaining. Hell, I wanted to build the man a statue or write him a song for what he did to my body.

When we got back to our seats, they were serving breakfast, and by then I was starving. Two rounds of hot sex and receiving two blow jobs seemed to wear me out!

While we ate, we talked about our lives, and I learned a lot about Amery. He lived on the outskirts of Colorado Springs by the airport and had a couple acres of land so no one would bother him or notice if he was practicing his magic.

He'd lived there and worked at one of the hospitals with a trauma center for twenty-five years. Which would have made me five when he got hired, but I tried to not focus on the age gap since it was normal in the paranormal world. And I could tell by the way he talked about his job that he loved it. Listening him go on and on about it, I found I was enthralled. He was a great storyteller and was so animated when he was excited.

"Are you tired? I can stop rambling now, and we can sleep," Amery offered as he glanced at his watch. "I mean, I've been talking for over an hour now."

"I can't sleep on a plane," I said with a shrug of my shoulders. "And I like listening to you talk about what you love. It's as if you live and breathe helping people. I find it fascinating."

"I've been told it's annoying because I don't know when to shut up," he replied quietly as his cheeks flushed.

"Well, I'm not them, and if it ever does get to that point, I'll say something, but not mean like that." I reached over and stroked my hand down his cheek. "Someone or some ones have fucked with your pretty head, Amery. You're amazing and deserve everything in life. Fuck whoever won't appreciate you and treats you like less than they should."

"I'm going to fall in love with you, Kirby." He looked scared shitless at the idea.

"I sure hope so or this will be a very long eternity together," I said with a smile. "I'll protect your heart if you do the same with mine."

"Deal," Amery replied and then kissed my palm with a smile.

We went back to talking then, leaning on our sides in the seats so that our knees were touching. As we sat there and learned about each other, we gently caressed each other here and there. I don't know about Amery, but for me it was more making sure he was real. Here sat the man of my dreams, loving, tender, hot, and off the charts in bed. And he was all mine.

# Chapter 4

Over the next week, I got settled into my new home and got used to waking up to a gorgeous man. And was he insatiable! We were having sex morning, noon, and night. Even after he went back to work.

I got my stuff packed up and shipped by a friend from my troop back in Orlando. I'd officially severed ties with them, and my Alpha had wished me luck though he admitted the troop would miss me. I was very active in our group of monkey shifters, and while I knew I'd miss some of them, I had a mate now. And I could always make friends here.

Everything was going great. Three days after we got home, Amery had to work the next four, and I met him every day for lunch. I'd make sandwiches and head over to the hospital. A few times we snuck off to one of the on-call rooms and made out like the teenagers I'd seen on television. Who knew hospital staff really did things like that?

We'd just finished lunch, and I was walking in the parking lot back to my car that I'd had shipped out to Colorado Springs, when something made the hair on the back of my neck stand up. I glanced around but didn't see anyone. It was strange, but it was like some sixth sense was telling me to watch out. I tried to shake the feeling off. It didn't work.

I walked along a few more cars before ducking behind a huge Dodge Ram. I shifted, grabbed my clothes, and hid under the truck. After a few moments I saw a big man's legs walk past the truck and keep going. That must have been who I felt, but why hadn't I seen

him then? I heard a car start up and pull out, so I guess he wasn't
following me or waiting for me.

Maybe I was being silly, but sometimes I just had to listen to my
gut when I felt something wrong. I crawled out, shifted back to
human form, and quickly re-dressed. I *really* didn't want to get
arrested for indecent exposure and have to explain to Amery why I
was naked in the parking lot of his hospital.

I shrugged off the incident without another thought and headed to
the grocery store. The night before, I'd gotten Amery to admit a few
of his favorite meals to me and decided to make something nice since
it was a week since we'd mated. I liked appreciating the little things
in life like that.

Once in the store, I realized I was whistling a happy tune as I
picked out vegetables for a salad. I paused for a moment and thought
about that. I *was* happy. Amery was everything I'd ever hoped for in a
mate, and things were going great.

I found what I needed for the beef stroganoff, grabbed a few more
things we needed, paid, and loaded up the car. Driving home, I
thought about the article I needed to write on the UPAC gathering.
Amery had helped me unpack and set up one of the spare rooms as an
office for me, which I thought was incredibly sweet.

He was so interested in my work it embarrassed me. I'd never
really had anyone I wanted to impress before. I mean, my mom was
proud of me, but I'd never cared what my partner thought of my
work. Until Amery. I cared about what Amery thought of everything,
but wasn't that how it should be with a mate?

I pulled into our driveway, grabbed the bags of groceries, locked
the car, and headed into the house. My phone rang with an unlisted
number as I was putting everything away. I answered it, but no one
spoke. Glancing at my cell, I saw the call was still going.

"Hello?" But no reply. Probably some stupid automated
telemarketing system that wasn't working. I hung up and slipped the
phone in my pocket. Then I got everything for dinner in the slow

cooker and headed up to the office. I sat down, booted up my laptop, checked my emails, and then started writing.

"Kirby?" Amery called out as I heard the door to the garage close. Looking over at the clock, I saw I'd been working for hours without so much as taking a bathroom break.

"In the office, I'll come to you," I yelled back. I stood slowly, my back popping as my spine adjusted from being seated so long in one spot. Then I saved my work and jogged downstairs. I froze when I saw the worried look on Amery's face. "What happened?"

"I've got something to tell you, but I'm scared at how you'll react or pass out again."

"You're pregnant," I gasped, having pieced together why he thought I'd faint. Amery nodded and took a hesitant step to me. I, on the other hand, raced over to him and leapt into his big arms. He grunted in surprise as he caught me just in time. "This is fantastic!"

"Really? You're okay with this?" he whispered as his body shook.

"I'm *thrilled*, Amery," I gushed, burying my face in his neck. "We're going to be daddies!"

"Oh thank the gods," Amery said with a sigh. "I know you said you wanted this, but when I found out I really was, I couldn't help but worry."

"I'll never lie to you or just tell you what I think you want to hear." I shimmied down his body, which had his eyebrows scrunching together. "I can't hop up on you like a monkey while you're pregnant. I could accidently kick the baby or something when I jump you."

"And you were worried about being a parent," he replied with a soft smile and cupped my cheek. "What smells so good?"

"I made us a nice dinner in the slow cooker to celebrate us being mated and me having lived with you for a week. But now we have bigger things to celebrate."

"I think it's great you got excited and planned this for our week anniversary." Amery smiled like a loon as he went to the cabinet and grabbed plates while I stirred dinner. I held out a spoonful for him to try. "Mmm, you're a great cook! I didn't know that."

"I don't know how to make much, but what I do know how to make doesn't get any complaints," I said with a giggle. He gave me a wink and set the table as I got the salad together. It was all so normal.

"I told the hospital I needed a maternity leave."

"Do they know that you're a witch? I mean, are you out as a paranormal at work?"

"I wasn't officially, though some people knew," he answered with a shrug. "Everyone does now, and there didn't seem to be any issues. I mean, I have been working there for twenty-five years. I'm sure most of them knew something was up though since I've not aged."

"I guess," I hedged, not sure if that was a smart move.

"What?" Amery stopped setting the table and stared at me as I chopped the vegetables.

"I know there are laws protecting paranormals and all of that," I started to say, choosing my words carefully. "But we did a spread a few months ago at *Sups Weekly* about stories of people who came out, and you wouldn't believe what some people went through. And I'm not just talking in small towns, Amery. There was a circuit court judge in New York City who was let go and a bunch of his old cases called into question."

"That's horrible," he gasped and plopped down into one of the kitchen table chairs. "I had no idea. I mean, how can that happen with the *Paranormal Rights* laws in place to protect us?"

"They came up with some bullshit reason other than the guy being a werewolf. But he had an exemplary record and years of service, and days after he came out he was suddenly fired for some crap that should have just been a warning. He didn't even do it and is still fighting his dismissal in court."

"I'm sorry, I wasn't thinking," Amery said sadly as he hung his head in shame. Shit! I raced around the island and knelt in front of him.

"You have *nothing* to be sorry for." I took his hands in mine in a show of support. "We should be able to be who we are without any repercussions, but that's just not how the world works. I mean, humans know about us, but knowing and accepting are still two different things. I think it's great you were honest. I just wanted you to know that there could be backlash and to be careful."

"Thanks for telling me," he replied with a weak smile.

"I didn't mean to be a downer on our great news," I said as I stood and straddled his lap. I threw my arms around his neck and gave him a deep kiss. "We can talk about reality later. Right now I want to revel in this moment."

"Me, too," Amery whispered against my lips.

We kissed a little longer with loving, soft kisses. Something else was eating at me though. I wanted to tell Amery that I loved him. I thought I did. I was pretty sure I did, but there was this voice in my head saying I wasn't completely sure yet. But Amery was having my baby. Shouldn't I tell him that I loved him? Isn't that what I should do with this news?

"It's okay, baby," he said softly as he nuzzled my face. "I know what you're thinking. I can almost taste your need to confess what's in your heart before you're ready. It's all over your face."

"You do?" I asked, completely shocked that I was so transparent when I thought I'd been hiding it.

"Yeah, I feel it, too, okay? We're just not there yet, but we will be. I know I'm falling so fast for you that I could say it, but I'm just not ready yet."

"You're not mad I can't say it when you're giving me the greatest gift ever?"

"No, Kirby," Amery answered as he rubbed my back. "This is all moving so quickly, and our emotions need time. I know how much you care for me, and that's more than enough for now."

"You have no idea how wonderful you are," I said with a sigh as I laid my head on his shoulder.

"You make me feel as if I am. I've never had anyone treat me with such love and respect before. I feel like a man worthy of love."

"You *are*, Amery. I wish just for one day you could see yourself how I see you."

"I'm getting there," he said as I leaned back to look him in the eyes. I saw his emotions and love for me shining in his eyes so brightly I thought I should grab my sunglasses, but it warmed my heart to see that look directed at me. "I didn't realize that I was broken or mistreated until I met you. You make me want to be a better man."

"You do the same for me," I replied honestly. I gave him a quick peck on the lips and got off of his lap. "Dinner's going to burn if I don't finish it, and we have to make sure you're fed. You're eating for two now."

"Yeah, I am." Amery chuckled as he rubbed his flat stomach. "It's so crazy to me that there's a tiny clump of cells growing in here that will be a baby in a few months."

"I know, right?" I quickly finished the salad and tossed it with ranch dressing like Amery liked. I set it on the table and then turned off the slow cooker and put the beef stroganoff in a large bowl. "We're going to have to do some serious shopping and plan on the third bedroom for the nursery."

"Do you want to know if it's a boy or a girl when we can? Or should we wait for the birth?" I thought about that while we shoveled food in our mouths.

"I think I'd like to wait, but I'm good either way really."

"Me, too," Amery admitted with a smile. "It's like the baby will be an extra surprise then, and we won't get caught up on just buying everything pink or blue."

"Good point," I said with a nod. "I do think we should find out what we're having. I thought a lot about this and talked with my mom some. She reminded me that monkey-shifter babies can have very strange needs unlike humans or other supernaturals."

"Like what?"

"They can't have regular milk or formula," I answered with a sigh because I knew I was lacking what our baby might need. "It has to be breast milk from a monkey shifter. First thing our baby could need and I can't give it to them."

"Neither can I, Kirby," he said gently and took my hand in his. "After we're done eating I'll call my Elder and see what he says. I know we'll love this baby no matter if it's a monkey or witch, but you're right. We need to be prepared."

"I just keep putting a damper on our news tonight."

"No, you're being realistic and a good parent." Amery kissed my hand, and we went back to eating.

Then he switched topics and asked about my article and how it was coming along. How could someone not love a man like him? Here he was pregnant and was about to go through major changes emotionally, hormonally, and physically, but he still cared about my article.

I quickly gave him the rundown on what I was writing. People had been writing into the magazine like crazy with their stories even before we asked for them. One guy was a phoenix who almost died because they didn't read the rules that UPAC gave us when we registered our mating. They didn't know about having to consummate the mating every twenty-four hours. Actually, that made me think of something.

"We also need to ask about having sex while you're pregnant," I said suddenly, interrupting myself. "The rules say we have to have sex every day."

"Okay, add that to the list of questions." He chuckled.

We finished up eating and then started clearing the table. I gave Amery an evil look and started taking dishes out of his hand and hip checked him to sit back down.

"Umm, wanna tell me why I got that?"

"You're pregnant with an incredibly short gestation period," I answered after I set the dishes on the counter. I crossed my arms over my chest and raised an eyebrow, daring him to challenge me. "You're going to be working most of that time, and that's fine. You're an adult and a medical professional, so you should know your limits, and I'm not your parent."

"Good to—" Amery started to say softly. He looked almost like a scolded child, and I felt a little bad about that since he was making strides in being more self-confident. But he had to know right away that I wasn't going to budge on any of this.

"However," I said firmly, interrupting him. "That much time on your feet is *more* than enough. You also will be eating, sleeping, and resting for two with all the exertion being pregnant will have on your body. So you are not to be doing any chores or anything physical while carrying our child."

"Or you're going to do what?" he asked with some defiance. Not quite anger, but again, more like a stubborn child who wanted to rebel.

"I didn't realize I had to threaten you on this." I was shocked at how this conversation was turning. Obviously I wasn't handling this right. I quickly changed gears to something softer. "I wasn't threatening you, Amery. I'm explaining why I wanted you off your feet. I'm not messing around, and maybe I'm being a dick about this, but it's coming from a good place inside of me. There's nothing more important to me than you and our baby."

"Sorry, you're right," he sighed and opened his arms to me. I immediately went to him and sat down very gently on his lap so my back was to his chest. "I'm just feeling a little all over the place, and then you're talking about how things need to be, and it just kinda chapped my ass."

"Well, while I fully intend on making sure your fine ass isn't chapped later," I said with a snicker as I gave him a wink over my shoulder, "you're entitled to be moody and get a free pass whenever you're pregnant. Plus I was a little overbearing."

"I do like it when you get all Alpha male and take charge." He purred in my ear and moved his hips so I felt his erection against my ass. I couldn't bite back the moan fast enough.

"First we have some calls to make, and then I plan on showing you just how appreciative I am of the gift you're giving us."

"Promise?" He licked my neck seductively, and I shivered with lust.

"Oh yeah," I groaned. "I have plans for my wonderful mate tonight."

"Okay, you're the boss." He chuckled as we stood up.

"Good that you recognized that already." I gave him my firmest stare but then smirked. He walked out of the kitchen smiling, and as he went, my cock started leaking at the sight of his tight, firm ass moving in his hospital scrubs. Yum!

I shook myself out of my lustful haze and cleared the table. Then I pulled out my cell and called the one person I knew who would be as excited as I was…My mom.

"Didn't I already talk to you today?" She chuckled as a greeting when she answered the phone. I couldn't help the wide smile that spread over my face as I started the dishes.

"Well, if you don't want to know that you're going to be a grandma, I can call back another day."

"What?" My mom, Isabel, screeched so loudly I had to pull the phone away from my ear. "Are you serious? You got Amery pregnant already?"

My mom was also one of my best friends, so she was all caught up with everything and even knew my fears about possibly being a father so soon into a new mating.

"Yes, I'm serious." I giggled into the phone. "He told me tonight when he came home from work. He's calling his Elder right now to

find out some things we're going to need to know, like what we might
be having so we can prepare."

"You're going to need—"

"I know, which is the other reason I'm calling you." My mom,
always the practical one. Can't imagine where I got it from? "Is there
anyone you know or have a connection with that could get us
monkey-shifter breast milk? I'm sorely lacking in that area."

"But I find that's the only area," she said sweetly. "I'm so happy
for you, Kirby. This is truly a blessing and a great day."

"I think so, too, Mom." I heard her sniffle then and realized she
was crying. "Oh, don't cry. This is good news!"

"I know, I'm just so happy for you," she whispered. "You know I
never once had issue with you saying you were gay. I never cared.
But I couldn't help but wonder and wish that I'd still have
grandchildren one day. I hope you know that I'm going to spoil this
baby so rotten, and I'm going to fly out from Orlando so I can meet
your mate, too. Is he as happy as you are?"

"Yes, once he realized I was really excited about it."

"Well, of course you were!" she exclaimed, seeming taken aback.
"I didn't raise no fool."

"No, but I am a guy after all, and I think there's some genetic
predisposition that just makes us have our heads up our asses
sometimes."

"Without a doubt." She giggled. "But you're one of the good
ones. And you better be pampering your mate and taking good care of
him, or I'll be flying there with the sole purpose of smacking some
sense into you."

"I fully plan on it." I chuckled, my heart warming that she was so
instantly on my mate's side.

Amery came back into the kitchen as I finished up the dishes with
a pensive frown on his face. That wasn't comforting.

"Hey, Mom, let me go and we'll talk more later," I said into the phone while staring at him. "Amery just got off the phone, and he doesn't look too happy."

"Okay, baby," she replied gently. "Let me know when you guys know more and due dates so we can talk about when's best for me to come out there."

"You got it. Love you."

"Love you more."

"What's going on?" I asked softly after I'd hung up and walked around the kitchen island to Amery. He took my hand as he shook his head as if trying to clear his spiraling thoughts and led me out of the kitchen, up the stairs, and into our room.

"I'm not sure. I just need a minute to wrap my head around what Elder Flores said, and then I'll tell you, okay?"

"Of course, honey," I said gently. I gave his hand a squeeze and kissed his temple before letting go and giving him some privacy. While Amery was mulling over whatever was in his head, I decided to get on to phase two of the romantic evening I'd planned.

I went into the bathroom and started to fill the large garden tub with warm water and bath salts. Amery's house was great, but his bathroom was mind-boggling. It was all done in gorgeous undersea mosaics with a shower stall for two, dual sinks and vanities, with the tub complete with jets. This bathroom and house in general were designed with a mate in mind. Amery had thought of just about everything.

After I lit some scented candles I knew my mate liked, I checked the water temperature. Perfect. I turned off the tap and went to grab my mate.

He was still sitting on the edge of the bed looking lost, his head hanging down and clasped hands leaning on his knees. Without a word, I lifted his arms so I could get his shirt off. Amery looked confused but didn't resist. I guess he'd been so consumed with his thoughts he'd missed the bath running. Wow, that kind of scared me.

I placed soft kisses along the skin I exposed. Amery sighed and closed his eyes as I knelt down and took off his shoes. I rubbed his feet quickly to loosen some of the knots before we soaked in the tub. Then I moved to the tie of his scrub pants. I tapped his hip, and he got the idea and lifted his hips. I pulled down his pants and boxer briefs at once, and then he was sitting there, gloriously naked.

Amery's eyes had opened back up, and he was staring at me intently as I glanced between his face and massive, hard cock. I'd make sure to take care of his problem later, but now was about some tender loving care. I took his hand in mine, tugging on it so he got the idea to stand, and led him into the bathroom. He smiled, and his eyes filled with tears when he realized what I'd done.

He went to say something, but I put one finger over his lips, and he licked it seductively. I moved my hands over his firm ass and guided him into the bath. He got in and sat down, all the while looking at me questioningly. I slowly undressed, making sure he got his fill of my soft skin I knew he loved so much. I also put a little extra sway in my hips as I moved to him and joined him in the tub.

I knelt down in front of him, grabbing a washcloth and bodywash. Amery's eyes were fixated on my movements as I poured some bodywash on the cloth and sudsed it up. Then I leaned forward and started washing his upper body. He let out a long groan as I massaged as I went. I felt his muscles relaxing under my attention, and I did my best to focus on him rather than his erection that was poking out of the water and tempting me.

Working my way down his body, I used my soaped-up hands and gently started to stroke his cock. Then I reached down with my other hand and squeezed his sac.

"Kirby," he gasped, his eyes going wide as I moved faster.

"Relax, my mate," I whispered gently as I leaned closer to him. His head fell back against the side of the tub as I sucked his nipple between my lips. Amery's hips started to move slightly in time with my strokes. I bit down, and he cried out my name. His warm cum shot all over my hand and stomach, but I kept working his body like a finely tuned instrument.

When I'd gotten all of his seed milked from his hot body, he sank further into the tub like a boneless heap. I smiled and kissed his lips as I let his still-mostly hard dick go. Then I moved him enough so I could get behind him and washed his back. After that was done, I tilted his head back and reached for the shampoo. I washed his hair, making sure to give his scalp a nice massage as I went.

It was perfect. Whatever had been worrying Amery seemed to disappear or at least become easier for him to deal with for now. He melted against me, and I placed soft kisses along his neck and shoulders as we lay there together and simply enjoyed each other. I was going to have to break the spell soon and find out what he learned, but for right then, in that moment, this was what we both needed.

# Chapter 5

"Elder Flores said he didn't know for sure what we'd have," Amery whispered, his voice sounding choked with emotion. "He did tell me that pervious cross matings he knew of resulted in multiple births, whereas witches normally only have one child at a time like humans."

"Is that why you were so upset, honey?" I asked gently as I ran my hands over his firm, very muscular chest. He nodded as he sniffled, and I could almost feel his fear. "So you are scared that I was okay with one baby but not two?"

"He said probably three," Amery whispered and turned in my arms. Sure enough, he was so afraid that his features radiated it. "One monkey, one witch, and one hybrid of both."

"Then we'll be three times blessed," I said firmly but with a smile. I realized it was the honest truth. Yeah, having three babies was a lot more work and complication than one, but it was still a great blessing.

"You're not upset?" he asked, his gaze raking over my face with a glimmer of hope.

"Scared, but no, not upset." I brushed my lips over his, and he relaxed. "Mom will help get us what we need for the babies, and we're not without resources, honey. I make a good living, and we can hire help if we need. We're together completely, and we're going to love these babies. My mom was asking when she could fly out to meet you and be here to help. We're not even alone in this if we don't want to be."

"You're amazing, Kirby," he whispered as he cupped my cheek. "You planned this whole evening for me, gave me space to think without issue, and you're taking this so much better than I did. I'm scared out of my ever-loving mind. What if we can't handle three? And who knows if it's three? What if we have four or five?"

"Then we'll buy more cribs," I said with a smile. "We can do this, Amery."

"You're sure?" He didn't look convinced but less scared.

"Nope, but I believe we can. I won't lie and say that this is going to be easy and I don't have any doubts, but I believe in us. And I think you're feeling overwhelmed, hormonal, and completely emotional. All of that is to be expected. But I think there is something you're not telling me that's bugging you."

"It's silly," Amery replied and sat back in the tub so we were facing each other.

"I'll be the judge of that," I said firmly and raised an eyebrow at him.

"What if you don't want me anymore when I get fat? I mean, especially with three, I'm going to get as big as a whale, and I know how much you like my flat stomach."

"Oh, sweetie." I chuckled and moved closer to him. I knelt between his thighs and took his face in my hands. "Yes, I think you have the body of a god, and it gets me hot." He flinched and went to pull away. "But that's not why I'm falling for you, Amery. You're more than my wet dream to me. And you're not going to be fat. You're pregnant, honey. The weight will come back off."

"What about when my stomach's so big I can't see my dick?"

"Then I'll kneel down, worship it, and take pictures for you so you know it's just as glorious."

"And if I'm not in the mood for sex?"

"I'll just have to massage your feet and take good care of my mate. What did Elder Flores say about the rules of consummation?"

"He said the magic of the spell recognizes when someone's pregnant and will automatically give reprieve. We have a few weeks after I give birth as well."

"Then that's one less thing to worry about, and we can just have sex when you're in the mood."

"And if I'm in the mood now?" he asked, his eyes dilating with lust as he licked his lips.

"It's okay for the babies if I penetrate you? Or should I bottom for the duration?"

"I'm fine for the first two months, and then I'll just have to take you when the mood strikes." Amery leaned in and gave me a soft kiss. "Make love to me?"

"Oh yeah," I purred and then stood. He took my hand with a big smile. We dried off and drained the tub before getting into bed. I took my mate slow and sweet until we reached our orgasms together. I was happy with the way phase three had gone. Very, very happy.

After I was done cleaning us both up, I got out of bed while Amery glanced at me with raised eyebrows. I gave him a wink of assurance and headed to my office to grab my laptop. Then I snuggled back in bed with him, our backs leaning against the headboard, and pulled up a few sites.

"You just think of everything, don't you?"

"I try." I chuckled as he snuggled closer against my shoulder.

First thing we did was order some parenting and baby name books from Amazon. Then we signed up for a parenting and birthing class at the hospital Amery worked at. Lastly, I pulled up one of those baby store chains that had nursery-planning software.

"I liked the green," Amery said as I flipped through options. We picked out the furniture we wanted and registered since my mate told me the nurses at the hospital loved throwing baby showers.

"Can I ask you something?"

"Of course, baby," he answered as he pointed out something else for me to pick.

"Where are your parents?" I cringed when Amery drew in a shaky breath. Obviously this wasn't a good topic for my mate. I swear I was subconsciously trying to sabotage this evening. I wanted to smack myself upside the head for causing him stress after I'd just spent so much time relaxing and spoiling him.

"I don't know, to be honest," he said softly as I closed the laptop and set it on the nightstand. I moved back to where I was and smiled when he laid his head on my chest. I stopped smiling when I realized he was shaking. "Witches are born the way they are just like shifters or vamps. But like any species, even humans, not all are good. There are witches who practice dark or black magic."

"This isn't going to be a happy story, is it?"

"No, not even a little bit."

"We don't have to talk about it if you don't want to, honey." I hugged him close and ran my hand over his back in a soothing manner.

"It's better to just get it out so you know what kind of family you've mated into."

"Fuck your family. I mated you, and you are your own person. Nothing they did changes who you are or reflects on the person you are."

"There are lots of people who think different," he said with a sad sigh. "That's why I'll never be a coven leader or even an Elder. It's also why I don't have a coven and live alone an hour away from any coven."

"I wondered why Elder Flores couldn't undo your gift of hemorrhoids even though he was Elder. You're older than all of the other witches that are in power. That is why they really fear you, Amery. It might have been your family ties in the past but now you're just fucking powerful."

"I honestly have no desire to lead. Maybe that would have been different if I'd not grown up the way I had, but some things you just can't change."

"I hear ya on that," I said sadly, thinking of the tragedy in my own life. Right now was about my mate though. We could talk about me later. "So your parents weren't the nicest people?"

"That's an understatement," he snorted angrily. "As a child, I had no idea how wrong what they were doing was of course. But I think part of me, no matter that they were my parents, knew something was off."

"Like what?" I knew he needed to get this out, and I was more than willing to guide him along if that helped.

"Human sacrifices," Amery whispered. "Black magic can be more powerful than regular magic, but since it's so dark and draws from outside sources instead of internal power, it requires sacrifices. It also upsets the balance of nature and can drive the wielder insane."

"You witnessed this?" I gasped, unable to hold it inside. "How old were you?"

"Ever since I can remember, honestly." I cringed for my mate. I'm not even sure my mind could picture the horrors he'd obviously gone through. "I remember hiding under the bed when I was about six because there was a human woman screaming in the ritual room my parents had. When the horrid noise stopped, I went to check that everyone was okay. I found my parents and other people in the dark coven having a blood orgy. The human was dead."

"Jesus, Amery," I said, my voice filled with sorrow for the child he'd been and the man lying here with me. I had a feeling the sins of his parents had landed on his shoulders and that's why he was so unsure of himself most of the time.

"Yeah, and I wish I could say that was the only time, but it just wasn't. And honestly, I'm pretty sure they never wanted me. They never hit me or beat me, but they just didn't seem to care about me one way or another. I was almost invisible to them."

"They obviously didn't have any morals, so why not just give you up?"

"Believe it or not, there are just some rules witches don't break," he said with a bitter laugh. "Abandoning a child, or giving them up for selfish reasons, tarnishes a witch's power, almost like giving themselves a handicap. I think they weren't willing to risk that it could really happen."

"I'd think giving you to another coven or couple would have been the most selfless thing they could have done instead of subjecting you to that."

"I honestly never thought about it that way," Amery replied slowly as if trying to think through what I'd said. "It makes sense, but I think they would have had to think of anyone else but themselves and their power for that to have crossed their minds. I was too young and scared to know what to do besides keep out of their way and hide."

"So what happened to them?"

"When I was fourteen, a few covens banded together to overthrow my parents' coven. They were quite merciless, though I can't say I blamed them. When I was older, I learned my parents had been threatening them and demanding money from other covens around where we lived in Ireland. My parents were able to escape, and I never saw them again. The covens killed everyone else and actually were about to burn me with them when one woman helped me escape."

"But you were just a kid!" I exclaimed in shock. "How could they throw you in with the rest of your coven?"

"When I was young, it wasn't like now, Kirby. We're talking over two millennia ago. At fourteen, I was an adult."

"So what happened then?" I asked, completely enthralled with the story. I had to keep reminding myself that this wasn't some mystery book I was reading. This was what my mate had lived through.

"I escaped and looted my parents' house before the covens found out. I grabbed whatever I could, focusing on the most valuable things so I could barter for what I'd need to survive. I had a late growth spurt, so I was actually about your size then and didn't have your shifter strength, so it honestly wasn't much.

"I knew they thought I was innocent of the sacrifices and black magic, but they thought, since I was so close in proximity to the magical influx of power those spells caused, that it had tainted me. That and it could have made me much more powerful than most witches. They thought that I might seek retribution for my parents one day and they'd be helpless to stop me."

"So they basically were trying to take you out of the picture on the chance you might want to do the same in the distant future? That doesn't seem right."

"No, it's not, but each town or tribe back then had their own laws. It wasn't like I could call the police and tell them what was going on. Hell, there wasn't even a UPAC or Elders then."

"Where did you run to?" I placed a few soft kisses on his hair and then temple to remind him I was right here with him and it was simply a memory.

"What's now London," he said with a sigh and rubbed his cheek against my naked chest. "I lived there for centuries, moving every decade to a different village so no one noticed I didn't get any older. It's not like nowadays where people just think what they want and probably assume I've had cosmetic surgery since I've not aged and worked at the hospital for twenty-five years.

"And then after a few centuries, I'd accumulated enough wealth to build a house in a more reclusive part of the country. After some more time, I hooked up with a coven that was smaller and wasn't a part of what happened to my parents."

"At least you weren't alone anymore," I replied, hopeful his tale got better from here on out. I couldn't have been more wrong.

"Yeah, but I wish I had been," he whispered, and I felt my chest get wet from his tears. I wrapped both arms around him and tried to push all my strength into him since he seemed to need all the help he could get.

"What did they do to you?"

"I was a powerful witch even then when I'd just started. I don't know if the covens that killed my parents' coven were right or if I just came from a strong linage. I was able to complete more complicated spells than someone of my little knowledge should have been able to. And the coven I was with was a very primitive coven that wasn't even up on the times way back then. They believed copulating was a way to gain power, especially with someone stronger than them."

"So you had a lot of sex," I said with a shrug, not really getting the problem.

"Not by choice, Kirby. Most witches had sex with humans, thinking they could draw life force power from them. The witches of that coven didn't have sex with each other because they thought they would then be *giving* their power up instead of taking the other's power. They weren't willing for one to come out ahead of the other and not have an even exchange."

"Shit, Amery," I gasped as hot tears filled my own eyes. How could I not cry after listening to all the pain my mate had gone through? And it wasn't even over yet. "How long did that go on for? How did it start?"

"At first everyone was really nice to me," he said with a shrug. "I knew how they felt about sex, but I was still a virgin and didn't want to embrace that side of their ways."

"You were a virgin?" I was adding up the years in my head and guessed he had to be about one hundred and fifty at least by then.

"Didn't want to get close to anyone and was practically scared of my own shadow. So yeah, I'd never even been kissed by then. Plus, I knew women didn't do it for me, and unless you were royalty and could pay hush money, being gay wasn't an option."

"Right, right," I replied with a nod. Damn, this was all a lot to wrap my brain around. I kept forgetting this was around the time of the Christians' Jesus Christ and nowhere near what life was like now.

"After I trained a bit and they realized how much power I had, the next full moon they drugged me. Next thing I knew I was tied down on a low altar and everyone of age in the coven raped me that night and every full moon after. They thought they had to give me time in between orgies to recharge my batteries of power. And they thought I wouldn't take any of their power from the sex since all of them were taking me and never letting me top."

"Kinda like how when I shift too many times in a short period, it takes me a day or so to feel back up to par."

"Yeah, any magic is draining, so they gave me the rest of the month off. I tried to escape, but they watched me like a hawk."

"This might be cold to ask, but I just have to know," I said slowly. I waited a couple of heartbeats, and then he nodded to go ahead. "Did it work? Did they actually become more powerful from the hell they put you through?"

"I think in their minds they did, like a placebo effect," Amery answered after a few moments. "They thought it would work, so in their minds it did. I never saw any real evidence that it worked, but then again, I was so lost in my own head and misery I can't say I'm a very objective source."

"Of course," I whispered into his hair. "I'm so sorry, Amery. You know none of that was your fault and you didn't deserve that, right?"

"I do now, but at the time I thought truly that I was paying for my sins."

"What sins?"

"All those human sacrifices that went on in my own home and I never did a thing, Kirby. I never stopped them or stood up for those poor people. I mean, I did try to tell someone once, but they went to talk to my parents, who of course denied everything, and they never let me out of the house again."

"Amery, you listen to me," I said firmly, moving so I could roll us over and stare into his eyes. It took him a second to open his up and focus on me, but he did, and I felt the shiver go through his body when he realized how upset I was. And I was…I was fuming.

How dare they fuck with his head like this and torment him! Not to mention the hell the other coven put him through by raping him. I shivered at the idea of how it all went down and my poor mate having to take on a whole coven.

"What your parents did is not your fault, and I admit I don't know squat about witches and magic. But I *do* know you well enough to say without a doubt that there's nothing evil inside of you. I don't for a second believe that your parents' black magic seeped into you somehow." I could hear the cold determination in my voice. All I wanted was for him to believe me.

"I've spent most of my life trying to prove that to myself," he whispered as I wiped away a stray tear. "I stopped fighting them and trying to leave, pretending that I was okay with what they were doing so they'd keep letting me train. I read everything I could on spells that could get me out of that hell. And I did every job around the village that helped me bulk up so I wasn't a scrawny, lanky tall guy anymore."

"You're a good person, Amery," I said gently. He wrapped his arms around me, and I nuzzled his neck as he continued.

"It took me a year to get to where I needed to be, but then I did something horrible, Kirby. I'm not as nice of a person as you think."

"What did you do?" I asked, making sure I sounded more secure that it wasn't as bad as what I was feeling inside.

"I did a stasis spell the day of the next full moon right before the orgy started," he said so quietly I barely heard him. "I froze them all for seven hours. I had already gathered some of their best spell books. I know it was wrong to steal, but I figured after almost two years of raping me and using me for what they wanted, I could take them as payment."

"That's no big deal."

"One of the men of the coven was strong enough to break my spell. I hadn't counted on how be-spelling twenty-five adults would weaken the hold on them so much. I was just loading up one of the horses when he attacked me. I grabbed my sword and killed him. I could have just wounded him, knocked him out, or something, but when I thought of all the times he hurt me, I just went crazy.

"Most of the coven wasn't mean when they raped me. I think most thought I actually enjoyed it since I came sometimes. My body responded from all the attention even when mentally I was dying inside. But he was evil, Kirby. He'd hurt me intentionally, tear me, beat me, and leave me bloodied and ready to die. And he always made sure he went last so by the time it was his turn, I was so weak I couldn't put up any fight and most everyone wasn't paying attention."

"He deserved his death and much worse, Amery."

"Wasn't for me to decide," he whispered and started shivering. I knew it wasn't from the temperature in the house. Some emotions just left a person so cold they felt it down to their very bones. I rolled over and pulled him to me so that we were in our original positions. "I killed that man, and since there was a freezing spell on the village, including him, I absorbed his powers."

"Did you know that would happen?"

"No, I had no clue," Amery said with a sigh.

"Then that's not the same as a blood sacrifice," I replied firmly. "He attacked you, and not just on that night. Courts have ruled self-defense for less than that, honey. You're still the wonderful man I know you are."

"This doesn't change how you feel about me?"

"I only respect you and care about you more. I can't imagine what you went through, honey, and you're a wonderful man. You deserve all the happiness in the world."

"After I left them, getting several hours head start, I decided to go into healing magic. I thought if I could save as many people as possible and help them, that I would make up for the life I took."

"I could see how you'd feel the need to make amends for what happened, but I think it's more than that." I rubbed my hands over his back and glanced down. He looked up at me with his eyebrows drawn together in question. "I think you are simply a good person, Amery. You have a big heart and want to help people. You might have mentally chalked it up as needing to use your power for good, but I think you would have done it anyways even if you didn't go through all of that."

"Maybe," he whispered and snuggled his head back down on my chest. He didn't sound very sure of that, but now wasn't the time to push his buttons. I felt his body relax, and I knew the time for learning more about my mate was over. He'd shared so much that anyone would feel like a used wet sponge after divulging all of that. "I've never told anyone all of that before."

"Thank you for trusting me. It means the world to me."

"I'll tell you another time why the current witches and Elders still don't trust me. But I have a question now."

"Of course, honey." I kissed his temple again, trying to let my caresses and love seep into my mate.

"What happened to your dad? You talk about your mom, but I've never heard you mention him."

"He and my mom weren't mates," I answered with a shrug. "They were a hook-up, and by the time my mom realized she was pregnant, he'd left town. I guess he was traveling or something. She said she tried to track him down so he'd know, but I get the feeling she didn't try all that hard or there's more to the story. For all I know, she never even knew his last name. It was the early eighties."

"Did you ever wonder about him?"

"Yeah, but more just in passing since I had so many male role models in our troop growing up. It was more that I wished my mom would find a mate and settle down. She deserves to be happy, especially after raising me on her own. I keep hoping now that she's only doing part-time work and helps the younger couples in the troop that maybe she'll find someone of her own."

"How come only part-time? Is she very old?"

"Naw, only like fifty, but I make enough money that I bought her a house a couple of years ago, so she doesn't have many expenses. I figured it's the least I could do after everything she sacrificed for me. Now she can focus on her for once in her life."

"You're such a sweetie," Amery whispered and tilted his head to kiss me. "I think that's wonderful that you did that for your mom."

I smiled down at him, my heart warming at his words and grateful we'd switched to better topics. What I'd learned that night about Amery made me understand why he acted the way he did much better than I did earlier today. Now I just needed to work on helping his wounds heal.

# Chapter 6

Over the next two weeks, Amery and I fell into a comfortable daily pattern. He didn't have a Monday-thru-Friday job, but then again neither did I, so we were great at being flexible. Since his position was mostly administrative as head of all the nurses in the hospital, he did work normal day shifts at least.

He'd get up before me on the days he worked, make the coffee, and we'd have a quick breakfast together. Then most days I brought him lunch and took a break from my work. And by the time he got home, I had dinner waiting, even if I cheated and did take-out a few times. Then we'd relax, talk about the babies, plan the nursery, and then make love until bed time. It was my own personal slice of heaven.

I did surprise him one day by painting the nursery before the weekend we said we were going to do it together. It wasn't hard work, and he was more than capable, but I was nervous about him being around paint fumes when carrying one or more of our babies.

He had gracefully taken the gesture in the way I'd meant it. And I was treated to some special thanks in the form of the best blow job ever and some toy play. I liked how my mate appreciated what I did and reciprocated. Oh yeah, did he ever thank me.

So I was shocked when I heard his car pull in the garage and then the front door slam closed at ten in the morning. I raced from my office, down the stairs, and skidded to a stop when I saw the look on Amery's face. To say he looked pissed off was probably the biggest understatement of the year.

"Amery? What happened, honey?" I asked hesitantly as I took a step forward and reached for him.

"Can't—" he answered through clenched teeth. "Not yet. Need first."

"What do you need?" His eyes flashed lust as he eyed over my body, and I got that he was trying to turn his rage into sex in an effort to calm down.

"You, Kirby. Need you," Amery growled and tore off his shirt. I nodded wordlessly as I took off my own shirt and moved closer. This might not have been the healthiest way to deal with whatever was going on in his head, but Amery wasn't supposed to be under any undue stress with being pregnant and all.

"You have me always, Amery," I said gently as I ran my hands over his smooth chest. He snarled at me, grabbed my shoulders, and spun me around so my face was pressing against the front door. I gasped in shock at how fast he moved and again when he literally tore my jeans off of me. I was glad I hadn't bothered with shoes that morning.

"Don't. You. Dare. Move." I shook in fear from the cold tone of his voice but nodded my head. It was turned to the side, so at least I could see over my shoulder as he went into the living room and retrieved the bottle of lube we kept there for when we needed each other and wouldn't make it to our room.

I was honestly more afraid of whatever news had set my mate off like this. I knew in my heart that the man I loved would never hurt me. It had hit me a couple of days ago that I did love Amery with my very soul, and I was dying to tell him. Now wasn't the time though. I got that.

Amery yanked off his pants and slipped out of his shoes as he made his way back to me. He leaned over and bit my shoulder hard, at the same time smacking my ass, causing me to jump from both points of pain.

"Who do you belong to?" he snarled in my ear. I was so shocked at his actions that I didn't answer immediately, and that earned me several more hard spanks that were so fast I barely registered them except for the stinging. "Why won't you say it? Who the *fuck* do you belong to for all eternity?"

"Amery Goddard," I cried as he shoved three fingers into my ass. It wasn't that I was against a little rough play during sex, and Amery had topped me last night, so I wasn't that tight. I was just frozen with shock and confusion at seeing this new, feral side of my mate. "I belong to you always, Amery!"

"Good answer," he moaned and mashed his mouth to mine in a brutal kiss that had our teeth banging together. "I'm sorry for this. Tell me to stop and I'll find another way to try and calm down. I just can't seem to control my rage and emotions."

"Don't be sorry," I gasped as he bit me again and pushed in a fourth finger before my ass was ready. "I'm here for you, honey. Take what you need from me. I can handle it."

"Thank you," he whispered and sniffled.

Okay, he went from red-rage angry to sniffling? Was this a hormonal pregnant thing?

"Shit," I hissed at his fingers being removed from me and his massive, hard cock slamming into me broke into my thoughts.

"Mine," he snarled as he thrust back into me hard. I didn't get a chance to reply as he grabbed my hips roughly and started pounding into my barely prepared hole. My body was flush against the door, so the angle was sharp and made my body tighter for him than normal, which seemed to break any semblance of control. "You're all I have left! And I will not give you up. You are mine forever!"

"Yes, Amery, all yours," I grunted out in between thrusts. I desperately wanted to move so my hands were bracing my body instead of my shoulders and my cock wasn't rubbing against the rough door. But I couldn't seem to get enough leverage under the onslaught of his much larger, much stronger body.

"Admit you love me!" he demanded as he fucked me even harder and faster. Damn, I didn't know he could even move like this. "I don't care if you're fucking lying right now. Just say it." Then he started punctuating his words with every hard thrust that almost had me crashing through the door. "Say. You. Love. Me. Now!"

"I love you," I shouted as part of my heart broke. I wasn't lying. It was how I truly felt, but this wasn't how I wanted to tell him. This wasn't the romantic moment I'd always dreamed of when my mate and I traded words of love. "I will never leave you, Amery. I will love you forever."

Amery roared out my name as he shot deep into my slightly battered body. He rode his climax as I stood perfectly still. Then he collapsed onto the door, smashing me in the process.

"I love you, too," he whispered as he moved slightly and nuzzled my neck. I swallowed back tears for sadness, confusion, and a little anger all rolled into one. Before I could say anything, much less figure out what I wanted to say, he pulled out of me and spun me around.

I moaned as he mashed his mouth back down to mine, much gentler this time. He lifted me up, and I instinctively wrapped my legs around his hips. Amery turned and pressed me against the wall adjacent to the door hard enough to knock one of the pictures down and items off the hall table.

He pushed back into me, and I was shocked he was still hard and ready to go. It's not like he had a long recovery time in between rounds, but this time I was pretty sure he never went soft. What was going on with him?

I didn't get a chance to ask as he started thrusting up into me hard and fast. Not as much as when I was up against the door but enough so I didn't really have a lot of air left for talking. And by now my cock and sac hurt so bad with need for release that I let out a pathetic whimper.

"Does my sweet mate need to come? Beg for it, baby," Amery said firmly in between kisses over where he'd bitten.

"Please, Amery. Please let me come. I hurt," I begged, whimpered, and pleaded with everything I had. He smiled wickedly at me and leaned forward so his extending stomach rubbed my cock just right. "Amery!"

"Good, mate, give me what I want." He purred in my ear. Oh boy did I ever. I came so hard that I thought the top of my head might shoot off. It felt like it would never end as I covered both of our stomachs with more seed than I thought my balls were able to hold. "I love you, Kirby."

And those simple words started a whole new orgasm in the middle of the one I was already having. Minutes or hours later, I'm not really sure which, I felt Amery go stiff and shout out his release as he filled my hole to the brink. I knew I should have felt guilty that I was enjoying this when he'd been so upset about something, but it was just too good to focus on much else.

"I'm so sorry, my love," Amery whispered against my neck a few moments later as his legs gave out, and he slid us to the floor. He seemed lost in himself and started to repeat it over and over. I gave him four times before it really just started to creep me out and went from gently rubbing his back to pushing away so I could see his face.

"What happened, honey? You have to talk to me because you're starting to really scare me."

"I–I got f–fired," he sputtered as his eyes started to overflow with tears.

"My gods, why?" I gasped in complete shock. And then it hit me like a ton of bricks. "Because you came out as a witch?"

"But they said I was stealing drugs," Amery said pathetically, seemingly completely crushed and nodded. "I would never do that, Kirby. I'm actually licensed as a physician and could get drugs if I wanted to. And it makes no sense where they said I supposedly stole them from."

"Explain that." I wasn't sure what he meant by that, and I had a feeling it was crucial information.

"Most employees only have access to certain supply closets and medical chests where we keep the prescription drugs. Like docs and nurses who work in pediatrics don't have access to neurology's supply."

"Okay, that makes sense. That would cut down on confusion."

"Right, and that was my damn idea years ago," he said with such venom in his voice I knew he was getting upset again. I rubbed my hands up his arms, and that seemed to calm him back down a bit. "I and only a few others have access to all the different areas because we're in charge of them or we rotate locations. I float a lot to fill in and check them all randomly to make sure their stock reports match."

"Again, seems logical." I gave him a weak smile, trying my best to show him I was on his side above all else.

"Well, the drugs stolen were a huge amount in oncology, which everyone knows I stay away from like the plague." Amery wouldn't meet my eyes then and turned a deep shade of red.

"So your ex-boyfriend works at the hospital?" I asked, rolling my eyes at how much more complicated this just got.

"Yeah, he's, umm, well, head of oncology."

"Figures," I groaned. "Okay, so this huge stash of drugs suddenly disappears and they linked that to you how?"

"Well, Jake's wife works there as well. That's how they met actually. She's a nurse in that ward."

"Let me guess," I started to say and then stopped to take a deep breath. I was ready to blow my top at the picture I was getting and those assholes hurting my mate. But it wouldn't do any good for both of us to blow right then, and my being upset would set Amery off again. "She just happened to report she saw you in there right before the drugs went missing?"

"I'm not sure if she was that specific. All I was told was that I'd been seen on that floor early yesterday, and she thought it was odd since I'm never there. And then the charge nurse went to get something later and saw their supply was wiped out."

"Did you tell them you're not an idiot?" I asked as I went to stand. We both groaned as his softening cock slipped out from me. I helped Amery on his feet and saw he was looking at me like I was growing another head. "Amery, if you *were* going to steal and you had access to all the different locations—why would you just clean out one place? You're smart enough to slowly steal a little from everywhere to throw the suspicion around."

"Yeah, I didn't really think about that," he said sadly as he plopped down onto one of the kitchen chairs. I went to the sink to wet a few paper towels. This was not a conversation to have while my mate's cum was leaking out of my ass. "I was just so floored that they thought I would actually steal. I've lived and breathed that place since it basically opened."

"Amery, honey, they don't think you stole shit," I replied gently as I wrung out the towels. I moved over to him and knelt in between his spread legs. I gently cleaned him up as I stared into his eyes. "I've got two really good guesses. Either they wanted you gone because of what you are or your ex-boyfriend is framing you. Have you guys been split up for long? Could he have found out you were pregnant and you never told him you could have babies?"

"Oh my gods," he gasped slowly. Light bulb! He never thought he was being set up. "I just thought there was a mistake or someone else stole them and I was a convenient scapegoat. You think Jake might have been behind this?"

I wanted to smack him upside the head. For someone as old as Amery was, he was also very, very naive at times. I guessed it was because of how he was raised and the way his own people shunned him that he didn't have much interpersonal smarts.

"I think right now you need to lie down and relax," I said as evenly as I could. I needed time to process, and my mate had had enough stress today, and I was worried about his body and emotional state. "I want you to take a nap before lunch, and we'll come up with a plan. Deal?"

"You're upset," he whispered as tears started to fill back up in his eyes. "I'm sorry I was so rough with you. I shouldn't have taken it out on you."

"I'm not going to lie and say I'm not pissed and hurt, though I want to so you will calm down and rest. But that's not why I'm upset, Amery. You gave me the option to say no, and I gave you the green light. Hell, I had one of the best orgasms of my life. I just might walk a little funny today and tomorrow."

"Then why?" he whimpered as I stood up. I shook my head, trying to think of what to say that might placate him until I had time to think without lying or stressing him out more. I grabbed some more paper towels after throwing out the other ones and cleaned myself up. "I'm sorry, Kirby. Please tell me what I did."

"For one, I think you should have maybe told me that your ex-boyfriend and his wife worked at the same hospital you do, especially given the way things ended. Plus, I've been going to visit you there almost every day you work, Amery. I could have bumped into him and been completely blindsided. Didn't you think he'd be pissed and direct it at me once he learned you were pregnant by another man?"

"I didn't think of that," he whispered and glanced down at his hands. I leaned my butt against the counter, really wishing we were dressed for this conversation. "I was pretty sure I should tell you, but I didn't know how you'd react, and things have been going so well I didn't want to upset you."

"I could give a flying fuck if he still works there because I know it's over between you. I *do* care that you've been keeping it from me, and it actually explains a lot. Did you change your emergency contact to me?"

"Yes, of course," Amery said with a sad, confused look that was pretty much an adorable pout that made me want to crawl on his lap and comfort him. And he didn't even know he was doing it, so that made it harder to ignore. "I don't get what that has to do with anything."

"I've been getting random hang-ups, and at least three times I swore someone was following me after I left the hospital. I told you this."

"Right, but I figured—"

"Figured what?" I practically growled.

"I heard a few female doctors talking about how hot you are, and I thought maybe one of them just kinda scouted you out for a better look or something. I assumed the hang-ups were wrong numbers or something." He shrugged and gave me puppy-dog eyes as if begging me to go back to comforting him.

"I need to think, and you need to lie down."

"You won't lie down with me?" His voice was so sad I felt like I was beating him. I shook my head again and walked way more calmly than I felt to our room. He followed after me, sitting on the bed and watching me as I threw on some clothes. I needed air, and I needed to not be there right then with him. "You're coming back though, right?

"Yes, Amery," I said gently. I went over to him and stood in between his legs. I moved my hand under his chin until he looked up at me. "I'll be honest. I'm not a fan of how we said we loved each other the first time. Those two things are what I'm upset about, but there is no reason to not come back home, because I *do* love you."

"I'm sorry," he replied and started to pull away. "I'm a horrible mate to you."

"You are *not*," I said firmly and grabbed his shoulders tightly to keep him from moving away. "I love you, and I'm coming back home. I need to think, and for a monkey, fresh air and the outdoors are the best way to do that. Please calm down and let me just think."

"Right, okay." He swallowed loudly and nodded as if trying to convince himself that I really would be back. "You've been more than patient with me, and I can give you some space. I don't mean to hover. I'm just scared and frustrated and hurt and confused and just about every other emotion swirling in my mind all at once. I swear I'm going crazy."

"You're not going crazy," I said gently and tapped his hip. He got the idea and moved so I could pull back the covers. I got him to crawl under them and get situated in bed. "You're hormonal and pregnant and have had your world shaken too many times in less than a month. Right now you need to chill out while I go take a walk. And then I'll bring home those sandwiches you like from the deli, and we'll talk."

"I do love you with all my heart, Kirby. I'm sorry that's how I told you for the first time."

"I know you are, honey." I leaned over and gave him a soft, chaste kiss before tucking him in. "Get some rest and I'll be home in a few hours."

"'Kay," he said with a yawn, and I knew he was exhausted, mentally and physically after two rounds of vigorous sex. I gave him one last look before leaving the room. On a whim I grabbed one of my many notebooks lying around my office and a pen. I knew once I sorted through a few things I was going to have questions, and I liked to be organized when I had this much shit on my mind.

I grabbed my keys and headed out. I honestly had no idea where I was going until I hopped on I-25 and saw the signs for the *Garden of the Gods*. Well, if that wasn't just a message from the powers that be, then I didn't know what was. I got off at that exit and followed the signs.

At first it was no big deal. Colorado Springs was one of the most picturesque places I'd ever seen, with mountains and nature surrounding the city. But as I got closer, I saw the most awe-inspiring rock formations that I didn't even know could exist. I parked at the main parking lot and got out of my car. I knew I probably looked like a goober with my mouth hanging open, but it was just so beautiful.

I walked for a good twenty minutes as I turned over everything Amery had told me. For now I would ignore my feelings about how we admitted we loved each other because that was something we could work through. The bigger issue was the pain and betrayal he was feeling right now.

I got about halfway through the main part of the park and plopped down on a bench. Damn, I was tired. It wasn't a level walk at all. There were hills and slopes that had me wishing I was in better shape. Plus, I was still adjusting to the altitude change of living here versus Orlando. Living somewhere surrounded by mountains will make a person realize they're out of shape though.

As I sat there, I started jotting down questions for Amery. And while I knew there was a way to prove he was innocent, I wasn't as concerned with getting his job back as I was clearing his name. If the hospital reported this to any officials, my mate could be at risk of losing his medical licenses. And no matter what, I was *not* going to allow that to happen.

I just didn't see Amery wanting to go back to work at the hospital once the dust settled and I handed a few of them their asses. He was big on trust, and I was pretty sure after all of this he'd never trust them again. This was a pretty big betrayal after all. They didn't even seem to have a formal inquiry or even suspension. I thought jumping right to firing was a pretty damn big "fuck off, witch" from the administration.

My only wonder was if this was a complete conspiracy or if they had help from Jake. I had a feeling there was so much more going on there than either of us knew. I mean, who fires a wonderful employee and Chief Nursing Officer after twenty-five years of employment from hearsay?

I pulled out my phone and made a few calls. I needed a few outside answers before I came up with a plan. I got one big fat lead from one of the main and most powerful Elders of UPAC. Elder Rice promised to talk to one of his herbivores and get back to me.

An hour later I felt confident I not only had a plan to clear Amery's name but also to figure out where he went from here. Because even as Amery's mate, I didn't want him going back to that fucking hospital. If they would stab him in the back like this, then they didn't deserve him.

I jotted down a few more notes and questions before making one last call to my editor as I headed back to my car. That one went even better than I could have imagined and left me smiling as I drove back home. Yeah, I saw the *Garden of the Gods* becoming my normal place to think and commune with nature when I needed inspiration.

As I drove to the exit, I almost dropped the phone a few times from the sights. There were several large rock formations that I couldn't believe hadn't fallen over yet. How they hell did they stay upright without braces or something? Plus, I just loved the way red rock looked.

I hung up with my editor as I pulled into the deli and got my mate his favorite comfort food. I also made sure to get an extra pickle and chocolate cookie since I knew he needed some extra smiles right then. After I paid and was driving back home, I realized in a roundabout way what happened to Amery might have been a blessing for him and all paranormals in the tri-state area.

# Chapter 7

I walked into the kitchen from the door off the garage and couldn't help smiling. My very gorgeous mate was in nothing but pajama pants, shaking his hips while making chocolate-covered bananas. It took me a second to recognize he was singing Gomez's "How We Operate," and gods help me, he was even sexier than when Owen sang it in *Grey's Anatomy* this season.

Right when the song lyrics were "turn me" he swirled around and froze. Guess he hadn't heard me!

"I was working on a way to say sorry," Amery said sheepishly as his cheeks turned bright red.

"Don't stop on my account." I smirked and leaned against the counter. "I was enjoying the show, and you have a great voice.

He stared at me a few moments and then blurted out, "I wasn't going to try and drug you with bananas so you jumped me or anything. I just thought after we made up—you said they were your favorite."

"I know, honey." I chuckled as I walked over to him and dropped lunch onto the kitchen table. Then I took his hand in mine and slowly licked the warm, melted chocolate off his fingers slowly as I held his gaze.

"I'm gonna cream in my pants." He groaned but didn't pull away.

"I'd like to see that."

"Does this mean I'm forgiven?" Amery swallowed loudly as I stared up at him. Was he? Did I work it all out?

"Yes. On one condition."

"Anything," he gasped as I released his hand and stepped away.

"I'm going to forget what we declared to each other during the sex," I said, holding up a hand when he went to interrupt me. "I still feel that way, but it killed me that that's how we said it to each other. So, in my mind we didn't, and that way we can do it right another time."

"Said what?"

"We said—" I started to reply and then realized he was saying it as way of acknowledging my request that it never happened. "Thank you."

"And everything else?" Gods, it tore at me how scared and lost he looked.

"Let's eat, and I've got some questions." He nodded and grabbed a couple of pops out of the fridge as I opened the bag and divided the food.

Amery was one of those almost too annoying people who were uber healthy. But during his pregnancy, he started craving sugar and pop like no one's business. I figured I got some reprieve then and we'd go back to unsweetened iced tea after he gave birth.

"Would Jake and or his wife have access to your personnel records and know you changed your emergency contact?"

"Yes," he answered immediately and then took a huge bite of his sandwich, looking away from me.

"Why are you looking away from me? Are you hiding something?"

"No!" he explained and inadvertently spit some roast beef at me. I couldn't help but snicker at that one. Amery chewed and swallowed quickly before trying again. "I didn't want to see you get annoyed at me for not having thought it might cause us problems."

"I'm past it, honey," I said gently, realizing while I'd settled a lot in my head with my outing, Amery hadn't and was still freaking out. "As long as you promise to never keep something like this from me again, we're good."

"I swear it to you, Kirby," he replied, looking years younger and as if a huge weight was lifted from his shoulders. "I was going to tell you. It's not like I was really hiding it. I just didn't know *how* to tell you, and things have been so great I didn't want my bullshit to fuck that up."

"But you see how not telling me could have screwed us way worse than just letting me know."

"Yes," Amery whispered and hung his head in shame. "Jake was always so jealous and freaked if I ever brought another man up."

"I'm not the jealous type really." I shrugged my shoulders. I wasn't. "And I trust you, honey."

"Really?"

"Of course," I said with wide eyes and then gestured to his distended stomach. "I'd never have children with someone I didn't trust!" He smiled then until I said what came next on my list of things to handle. "I called a civil rights attorney who works on paranormal cases. We've become really tight, and he knows a couple of judges still hiding what they are that help him from time to time when most judges would roll their eyes at his requests."

"W–why do I need a lawyer?" He looked like he was going to shit a brick.

"Amery, you were falsely accused of stealing and fired with no proof," I answered carefully, not wanting to upset him even more. "He's getting a court order right now for the hospital's security tapes, hopefully before they think to destroy them. You're pretty passive most of the time, and I'd bet they didn't plan you would fight this."

"I don't want my job back if this is how they're going to treat me."

"I know that." Shit, here came the next bomb I was guessing he didn't think of. "But stealing drugs is a really big accusation, honey. You could lose your medical license over it."

"The director of the hospital swore he wouldn't be pressing formal charges." Amery's eyes were the size of saucers.

"And that right there lets me know they have no proof and this is a bullshit charge." I took another bite of my sandwich and mulled that over while I chewed. "If they thought you really did it, they wouldn't want you to practice anywhere else ever."

"Yeah, I started to wonder about that when you went for your walk. This is such a fucking mess, Kirby."

"I know, but we can fix it." He looked so defeated I knew I'd do anything to wipe that look off his face, so I bit the bullet. "Amery?"

He looked up at me and we stared at each other for a moment.

"I love you," I whispered. "You are my everything already, and I can't imagine my life without you, don't want to. If I lived thousands of years, I couldn't have picked a more wonderful mate than the one UPAC tricked me into finding."

"I love you, too, Kirby." His eyes filled with tears, but he was smiling so widely I felt a lot of the pain and tension leave the room. "Thank you for calling your friend and helping me."

"Oh, I'm not done yet." I snickered, knowing full well I had more tricks up my sleeve. He gazed at me so questioningly that I elaborated. "Did you know UPAC has been looking into opening some paranormal clinics?" He shook his head and then his eyes went wide as he if caught my meaning.

"Me?" he squeaked.

"Yes, you. You've got centuries of medical experience with all types of people and so many licenses I don't even know what they all mean. You'd be perfect to open and run a clinic. We're close enough to Denver that people could easily get here, and we've got an international airport. I talked to Elder Rice of the herbivores about it, and he thought Colorado Springs would be a great location.

"He's got a research guy, Shea Mayer, who was looking to expand his lab company. And said he'd help fund one of the clinics if he could hire some techs that would help him on side projects when his staff got overwhelmed. We might not need full-time lab staff right in the beginning, so they wouldn't be getting paid to sit around and twiddle their thumbs."

"You've been very busy." He chuckled.

"I have, but I also have more," I said with a wink. "I do need to ask you some other things, starting with something I couldn't believe we've not talked about yet."

"Money, right?"

"Yeah!" I still couldn't get over that we'd been mated for three weeks and I had no idea about Amery's financial situation, nor did he know about mine more than I made a good living.

"Not ever a problem. Do you think I should fund the clinic and just get UPAC's seal of approval?"

My jaw practically hit the table at that one. He was talking about funding a clinic the way I'd think about buying a new DVD. That and he was switching into professional mode and acting all confident again, which was turning me on.

"Yes, I have lots of money." Amery chuckled and moved his fingers under my jaw to push it closed. "You're gonna catch flies that way, babe."

"You have enough to fund a clinic on a whim?" I blurted out with wide eyes. "How?"

"Oh, lots of different ways." He snickered, but then got serious. "All of them legal, Kirby. I never used black magic or anything."

"I never thought you would!" I said, letting my shock show in my words. "You'd never hurt people, Amery. I was just curious, but you don't have to tell me."

"No, I'm not hiding it, but after living a few thousand years there are so many different ways it would take me a week to list them all."

"Just give me one because I'm dying to know." I felt giddy. What cool stuff had my mate done over the years?

"Well, I can't say I was always legal actually," he said thoughtfully as he leaned back in his chair. "I was a pirate for a few decades and made a lot of money that way. But I didn't do it for the money. I was against slavery." Totally cool much? "I had money back then, even if I didn't flaunt it and act like some material douche bag. I bought a few fast ships and hired a few crews to help intercept slave boats as they came to America.

"I'd have some of the crew release them and get the poor kidnapped people back home, but we'd keep whatever else we pirated. There's actually a village still in southern Africa named Goddard after me. I sent men to build the place as a refuge for the displaced slaves."

"Holy shit!" I gasped.

"Then I'd turn around and sell the boat we stole to England or France. Oh, I used to help museums on digs in the early 1900s. I was alive when the civilizations were actually there, so I knew where the best ruins and relics would be. I would get a large finder's fee and commissions on what they found. I made several million dollars that way."

"How cool is your life?"

"Maybe," he said slowly, and then his eyes softened as he reached for my hand. "But I wasn't happy. I've never been happy really until I met you, Kirby."

"Me, too," I whispered as I squeezed his hand, trying not to get choked up on the emotions I felt. Then another idea hit me. "I was going to ask if I could interview you about the way the hospital treated you. I called my editor, and he wants to help and okayed the story, but I think, if it's all right with you, that we should do a whole spread. I never thought about how the older paranormals would know so much history!"

"You called your editor, UPAC, and a lawyer to help me while you were gone?" I nodded, worried he might be upset until I saw the warm smile cross his face. "You are, like, the best mate ever!"

"I'm glad you think so." I giggled, blushing under his praise. "Oh my gods!"

"What?" he asked, his eyes filling with excitement.

"I've had a few publishers ask me to write books on paranormals' stories, but I never really had the drive and was comfortable with what I was doing. Maybe we should do that? We could donate the proceeds into a fund to help set up other paranormal clinics. Do you have any idea how many don't ever seek basic medical because they're scared to be found out? That's how this whole idea started with UPAC."

"And you say that I'm such a kind man," he said and shook his head. Then he glanced up at me with so much love in his eyes that I felt it like a warm blanket. "You have no idea how amazing you are, Kirby. I help people medically, but I bet you never see how much you help them with your stories and writing."

"I guess I never thought of it that way," I replied with a shrug. "I just think people should know about the injustice in the world. I mean, how can it ever be changed or people know they're not alone if they don't know about it?"

I wanted to say more, but a knock at the door interrupted our conversation. I gestured for Amery to stay seated and jogged to see who it was. When I looked through the peep hole, I saw a well-dressed lady who didn't seem imposing. Boy, did I ever get that one wrong.

"May I help you?" I asked after I opened the door and moved over the doorsill. Before I could even register what was going on, she bitch slapped me.

"My husband is not coming back to that whore of a witch, so tell him to stop trying to steal him."

"Watch your mouth, bitch," I snarled and stepped closer to her. I guess she thought I wouldn't retaliate. What? Because she was a woman? Fuck that, she just assaulted me. "You show up at our home and insult my mate, not to mention accosting me. I'd be very careful of your next words because they might be your last."

"Oh please, you're like four feet tall," she scoffed, getting that snooty attitude back. Okay, fine, she had maybe five inches on me.

But seriously? Four feet? Come on now! "I could kick your ass with one hand tied behind my back.

"You'd think humans would stop assuming everyone else was human in the world nowadays." *That* got the reaction I wanted, and she swallowed loudly. "You have no idea what animal I turn into, and while I might be small, I'm way stronger than a human twice your size and much harder to kill."

"J–Just keep that witch away from my husband!"

"He doesn't *want* Jake," I snarled. "Jake's been starting trouble with us, lady—"

"What is the meaning of this, Yolanda?" Amery asked with a cold, even voice from over my shoulder. "Why are you here?"

"You stay away from Jake!" She took a step back though as she shouted, realizing she was out numbered. "You've fucked with his head now that he knows what you are and can have kids."

"That's not Amery's fault! Our mating and babies have *nothing* to do with you or Jake." I growled, feeling that our mating was being threatened.

"Right," she said as she popped her hip and put her hand on it dramatically. "Like you sick freaks wouldn't love to get someone else in your bed. Well, you can't have him."

"Fuck you! We don't want him, and you wouldn't be here if your man was straight," I shouted and got in her face. "Can't please him like a cock up his ass can? You're here because you're looking for someone to blame. Go blame your fucked-in-the-head husband."

"I'll kill you if you mess with us anymore," she yelled at Amery.

"Yolanda, I'm not doing—" Amery started to say, and I could hear the pain in his voice. Now she'd hit me, threatened us and to kill Amery and hurt him. I couldn't have stopped the shift if I wanted to. My monkey took over, and I changed right there on the front porch.

"You're a *monkey*?" She laughed and pointed. "You were threatening me about your big bad animal and you're a goddamn little monkey! You really are freaks."

I tilted my head after moving out of my clothes and felt an evil smile cross my face.

"You leave Kirby alone, Yolanda." Amery growled and stepped forward. "I've always been good to you, congratulated you when you got married to Jake because I liked you. And no matter my past issues with Jake, they had nothing to do with you, just like this has nothing to do with Kirby."

She went to raise her hand to smack Amery, and I knew, unlike me, he would never hit a woman. But that was my mate, and he was carrying my child. No fucking way!

So I did what any monkey does when threatened...I bared my teeth and threw poop at her. She screamed as if I'd stabbed her instead of launching shit at her face.

Okay, fine, it wasn't really poop. It was mud. But she didn't know that. All she was seeing was me reaching behind my back and launching brown stuff at her. She just didn't realize I was grabbing it from the planter I'd watered on the front porch this morning.

"You animal!" she screeched as I launched another handful. "You fucking demented animal."

"Leave now, Yolanda, and never come to our home again," Amery said firmly as he picked me up into his arms. "Take your anger at Jake out on Jake and tell him to leave us alone. I love Kirby, and we're happy together. I don't want Jake. I realize now I never loved him. I was just desperate for someone to love me. I have that now, and he's ten times the man Jake ever was."

"You're both sick," she sneered and then spun on her heel. We watched as she got into her car, mud all over her face and clothes, and peeled out of our driveway. I was snuggled in Amery's big arms, purring almost like a kitten as he stroked my fur gently. He did it like it was the most natural thing in the world, and I don't think he was even doing it consciously.

"Did you really just throw feces at her?" He chuckled and carried me back inside. I smiled my monkey smile at him until he set me down on the ground and went to close the front door. I shifted back then, sat there with my legs spread wide so he knew how much I really liked the petting.

"No, it was mud from the planter." I giggled. Amery busted out laughing as he flipped the dead bolt and then stopped just as suddenly when he turned around and saw my leaking erection.

"That turned you on?" he asked in a whisper as he stared at my cock.

"I defended and protected my mate," I answered with a sly smile. I reached down and started stroking myself as his eyes followed my hand's movements. "My monkey is dying to claim what is ours. But you also said a few things that warmed my heart and defended me, which turns the human side of me on."

"Want a banana?" He purred as he knelt down between my legs.

"If you give me one now with how horny I am now"—I moaned as he cupped my sac and rolled it in his hand—"I'll be buried in your ass for days."

"I'd like that," he whimpered and suddenly swooped me up into his arms and was on his feet. "I'd like that a lot."

I laughed like a loon as he raced to our room to collect on my offer. And to say we had hot monkey sex just doesn't seem to cover what happened in our bed for the next two hours.

\* \* \* \*

Just as we reemerged from our room after taking a nice tender shower together, my phone rang. Since Amery had moved my clothes into the living room when I shifted on the front porch, it was in my jeans downstairs. I raced down and answered it just in time.

"I have the tapes, and you won't believe this shit." My attorney friend Ralph growled in the phone. It never surprised me he was a werewolf from the amount of times he growled.

"And hello to you, my furry friend." I winked at Amery and then mouthed "lawyer" so he knew who I was talking to. He nodded and smiled, letting me know he appreciated the consideration.

"You're one to talk." Ralph snickered. "You got your laptop?"

"Yeah, hang on." I raced upstairs to grab it and then down into the living room where Amery was relaxing so he could see whatever Ralph was sending me, too. "Okay, booting it up."

"Let your mate know that I've already sent a copy of this to the medical board along with a brief report of what happened to him. So I'll let you guys know when I hear from them."

"You seriously don't screw around." I chuckled as I loaded the video he'd sent me in an e-mail. I heard Amery cry out as we watched a guy in a doctor's coat walk into a supply room and leave a few minutes later with his arms full of boxes and bottles of drugs. "Jake?"

"Yes," he whispered as tears streamed down his face. "They really set me up. This wasn't pointing the finger accidentally at the wrong person."

"I'm sorry, honey," I replied gently as I wrapped an arm around his hunched shoulders. I was going to feed Jake his balls and enjoy it for what he was putting my mate through. I tapped the button on my phone so Ralph was on speaker. "Ralph, I've got my mate Amery with me here."

"Hey, man, sorry you're getting screwed like this," Ralph said in his best "understanding professional" voice. "We're going to make this right."

"What next?" I asked when Amery simply nodded and didn't seem to be able to find words.

"Well, the hospital knows that we know this now, so my best guess is that they'll try and get Amery back and plead that it was all just a big mistake. But I say we file a suit for wrongful termination and paranormal prejudice so they see that we're serious."

"Okay, but I don't want the money," Amery said softly after a few moments of thought. "We can set up a clinic fund and put whatever we get there. Plus, Kirby was talking about writing a book or books to help as well."

"What are you writing about?" Ralph asked. He was a lawyer I'd met through the magazine and became fast friends with. "Need me to look over some contracts?"

"You're just full service," I teased with a smile. "My mate is thousands of years old and has some really cool stories about the history he lived through. I think they'd make for some fascinating books."

"UPAC in on setting up the clinic?"

"Elder Rice was going to let me know but said to call him once I had proof of Amery's innocence because that would really help get the ball rolling. He's been trying to get this idea going, but some Elders are still dragging their feet. But Amery and I haven't gotten much chance to talk about it, so we're not sure what's going on yet."

"All right, I'll leave you guys to it then. I look forward to meeting you soon, Amery. You take care of my fur-ball friend."

"I will," Amery said as he snuggled against me after I set the laptop on the coffee table. "I love him, and he's the best thing that's ever happened to me."

"Big words coming from someone who's lived as long as you have," Ralph replied with a tone of awe. We finished our good-byes and hung up. I thought about what Amery had said and Ralph's response. He was right. That was a *huge* compliment coming from someone as old as Amery. And damn if that didn't make me smile like an idiot for the rest of the day.

# Chapter 8

"And once we get the book through edits we can…" someone from the publishing house rambled while I signed my name.

But I wasn't listening. I was thinking about the past few weeks spent working on everything I'd started with my phone calls the day Amery got fired. Ralph had been right. The hospital had called the next day and begged Amery's forgiveness and even offered him a raise if he came back. What they *wouldn't* do was fire Jake. If that didn't scream conspiracy, I didn't know what did.

The medical board, however, wasn't as nice about it. They were going after the hospital and Jake for their licenses and taking criminal action. That made me feel much better about the people in charge of who was a licensed medical professional in this country.

"I gotta call Elder Rice and check on the last wire transfer,"

I mumbled as I finished up and pulled out my phone.

"Were you even listening to me?" she asked. I think she was the agent. No, the editor? Okay, so I might have been distracted, but I nodded that I had been paying attention as I thought about our biggest supporter in all of this.

Elder Rice had come through on the UPAC side. After Amery agreed to run the clinic if they approved it and I sent the proof of his innocence, the Elder had called us back with great news. UPAC had approved it, giving total funding for the construction of the building while that herbivore, Shea Mayer, would be supplying all the medical equipment.

That was the deal as long as Amery was the one running it and would oversee it all so they didn't have to send people to handle it. That and he'd do all the hiring of staff and doctors once it was built.

At least I'd found out why most of the Elders didn't like Amery besides his parents. It seems when he was younger and powerful he wasn't a fan of their snide comments. They really should have seen the hemorrhoids coming.

"Okay, thanks!" I said brightly and interrupted her again. "I've got a pregnant mate." I booked it out of there and sighed as I pictured Amery in my head.

My mate was over-the-moon thrilled at everything. Then my editor was just as thrilled when he found out we'd be giving him the exclusive story of all of this to help us find the right personnel.

We worked our tails off getting everything ready so construction could start right when Amery should be going into labor since he wouldn't be much help then anyways. There was finding land that we could buy, getting building permits, finding contractors, and on and on and on.

Plus, we were still preparing for the babies we were having. Which we found out there were four. Yes, four. We'd both had a slight meltdown when we learned that one. But in true mom-type fashion, mine had flown out the week before Amery was due to help with last-minute details. She'd also hooked us up with a contact from our troop that could get us the monkey breast milk we would need.

I was driving back from signing the book deal contracts. They based on the outlines I'd submitted for a story about the history Amery lived through when I got the call.

"It's time," my mom squealed in the phone.

"He's a day early!" I quickly flipped my turn signal and turned so I could get on I-25 to get to the hospital.

"Yeah, babies don't have calendars in there." She snickered.

"Isabel, tell Kirby I love him." I heard Amery in the background, sounding in way more pain then I wanted my mate to ever be in.

"I love him, too," I said before she could even relay it. "I'm about twenty minutes away, but I'll get there soon."

"Okay, kiddo. Just take a few deep breaths and don't get in an accident. I've been through this before and everything's going according to plan."

"Thanks, Mom," I replied and then we hung up. I took her advice to heart, relaxing as much as I could. But seriously, I thought now might be a good time to start smoking. Because I never had one cigarette in my life, but suddenly I thought maybe I should start. I mean, four babies. Holy shit!

I was still debating the concept and trying not to panic when I got to the parking lot twenty-five minutes later. Damn Friday afternoon traffic!

That's the only excuse I had for not paying attention to who and what was around me. I heard a sound and turned, but too late since something very hard smashed into my head. I wasn't sure, but I was pretty convinced it was metal because I went down like a ton of bricks and blacked out before I hit the pavement.

And then woke up sometime later in an abandoned building, chained to the wall. It took a few minutes for my eyes to adjust with the throbbing pain on the right side of my head. I felt as if my temple was going to pop out the other side.

"Those should be my children!" Jake screamed in my face. Yeah, that helped. I eyed the lunatic in front of me over since I'd only seen him in that video footage and a few pictures afterward in the papers. "He never told me he could give me children. That was the whole reason I married that viper. She could be a good doctor's wife and give me lots of babies. But the joke's always on me!"

"Oh my gods, she's infertile," I guessed from the venom in his voice. "That's perfect! People like you shouldn't be procreating anyways." I shivered at the idea. "And just for the record, you're a fucking moron."

"Really? And how would that be?" He sneered at me and was even uglier that way.

"Your wife tell you what kind of shifter I am?"

"Of course, though I can't trust what she says obviously," he answered, rolling his eyes. I wasn't sure if it was at me for bothering him in his righteous rant or because of her. I didn't really care.

"Then you're a fucking moron," I said again, holding up my hands in the chains. "These won't work, and as much as I'd love to stay and tell you everything I want to before I hand you your ass—*my* children are being born right now."

Without another word, I shifted. Any other day I would have laughed at his shocked face as the chains fell to the ground around me as I turned into a small spider monkey. Any other day I would have wanted to kick his ass and find out what he had been thinking. Any other day I would have traded insults until he was crying in the corner.

But this wasn't *any other day*. It was today, and I was missing the birth of my children and when Amery needed me most.

I gave the asshole a little salute and scurried out of the building. And found myself in downtown Colorado Springs. What an *idiot*! Yeah, he might have been smart enough to become a doctor, but what moron kidnaps someone and holds them in a populated area?

I found a police car within two minutes of my escape, though it was empty. People shouted and a few screamed as I hopped up on the hood, beat my chest, and cried out to get the officer's attention. Sure enough, seconds later one came racing toward me. I waited until he was standing next to the cruiser and then shifted back.

"I was kidnapped," I said, covering my groin with one hand while pointing to my blood-soaked head. "I know the guy who did it, and he took me to that building." I pointed behind me. "I know there's lots to be done and statements to be given, but I'll heal, and my children are being born. My mate is in the hospital in labor. Please take me to him!"

"Him?" the guy asked, his eyes going wide.

"Yes, he's a witch, and I'm a monkey." I really wanted to just speed this part up. Luckily, the gods were on my side right then.

"And I'm a vamp," he said, flashing fang quickly so only I could see. "So you're in luck today, little monkey."

"I was just thinking the same thing."

"Hold up, I've got some gym clothes in the trunk for my workout later," he said quickly as I started to get off the car. I nodded and waited, trying to ignore that my ass was on fire since the sun was out and had warmed the hood of the car, and I didn't think he'd been parked there that long.

He threw some shorts and a tank top at me while he got on the radio and relayed what was going on. I told him Jake's name and address so they could pick him up. And then we were on our way. I'd never been in a squad car before, but if it got me to Amery faster, I didn't care if I had to ride in the trunk.

I almost laughed when I realized that I was so excited and full of adrenaline that my head barely hurt anymore. It didn't take ten minutes to get us to the hospital with the sirens going. I leapt out of the car the second he opened the door for me, and I realized he was right on my heels as we raced through the hospital.

I got up to the maternity ward and was just approaching the nurses' station when I heard my name.

"Holy shit! Kirby, are you okay?" my mom asked as she ran to us. You couldn't miss my mom ever with her gorgeous, sleek, raven-black hair. She was as short as I was, but the woman was all woman with curves. It used to embarrass me when I was a kid that the other guys used to refer to my mom as having the same outrageous measurements as Barbie. Geez.

"I'll live, but how's Amery?"

"He's just getting ready to start pushing, so I stepped out into the hall to call you again. What the hell is going on?"

"I promise to explain everything as soon as our babies are here," I called over my shoulder as I booked it to the room she pointed to. "Thank you, officer!"

"I'll be here," the man called out. "We need to get your statement once you're done."

"Can you tell me why my boy is bleeding?" my mom asked the police officer in an icy voice. I could just imagine the man shaking under my mom's glare, but I didn't have time to watch right then.

"Okay, it's time to push, Amery," the doctor said as I threw open the door.

"Not until Kirby's here," Amery cried out as another contraction hit him.

"I'm here, my love," I said gently as I moved to the side of the bed.

"I'm going to kick you for being so late," he panted but looked worried. "I thought you were chickening out and running."

"Never," I replied firmly and leaned over to kiss his forehead. I took his hand in mine and smiled at him. "You ready?"

"Yes, but you're explaining that blood on your head the second I'm done."

"I'm fine and will tell you everything later." The doctor looked appalled as he watched us go back and forth. "Let's do this, doc."

He gave me a quick nod and snapped back to the task at hand. I learned that it had been over three hours since Jake had knocked me out, and I was glad Amery wasn't having one of those horridly long labors.

I found myself wanting to faint a few times at the pain my mate was going through, but I held on. Then again when I saw the *stuff* that came out of him when the first baby was pushed out...I call it stuff because I know there were terms for it, but seriously, I didn't want to know. Stuff just worked better for me right then.

One of the nurses standing by took our baby and announced it was a girl before cleaning her up. Amery pushed out three more, though how on earth he managed, I have no idea. When it was all done, we had two beautiful girls and two gorgeous boys. I cried like they did at the sight of them and when it was over and everyone was okay.

"I love you so much," I cooed at Amery, trying not to blubber all over him.

"I love you, too, Kirby," he said in an exhausted voice. "Did you get in an accident? Isabel's going to kick your ass if you did."

"No, I got here fine, but then Jake knocked me out and kidnapped me," I answered quietly. His eyes got wide, and I could see the hundred questions he wanted to ask floating in them. But I think right then all that mattered was that I was safe, and he was just too wiped. "He locked me up in chains, so when I woke up, I shifted and found a very nice police officer who got me here right away."

"I want to talk to this man right now," Amery demanded as two of our babies were placed into his arms. One was handed to me as well, and I nodded to my mate. Amery got whatever he wanted for a very long time. Plus, I wanted to let my mom know she was a grandma four times. We'd kept that part a secret and hid two of the extra cribs from her.

"Oh, grandma," I sang out as I stepped into the hall. My mom gasped and raced the few steps over to us. I saw the officer lurking and looking a little uncomfortable. I gestured with my head for him to come over as I handed over my son to my mom.

"Seriously? Most people wouldn't trust a vampire around their baby," the guy blurted out as he stepped over to us. I saw him glance at my son and then back to me. "He's a cute little bugger."

"I'm not most people, and I think you can control yourself." I chuckled and rolled my eyes. The way people thought of vampires cracked me up. Just because they drank blood didn't mean they'd attack anything with blood. I mean, humans ate cows, but did they take a bite out of them any time they saw one? Stupid stereotypes. "My mate would like a word with you."

He raised an eyebrow at me as I opened the door and ushered them both inside. It was a large birthing suite, so there was a couch and a chair along with more than enough room for the babies' cribs and the nurses.

"You're the man who saved my mate?" Amery asked as the officer approached his bed.

"He saved himself, sir." The guy snickered. I wondered about the respect, but then I guessed either it was from Amery having done what he couldn't by giving birth or he understood how much older my mate was than all of us. "I just gave him my workout clothes and a ride. He escaped on his own and started jumping on the hood of my cruiser in monkey form."

"Sounds like my man," Amery replied with a smile. "What's your name?"

"Officer Moran, Kyle Moran," he answered as he stared at the babies. "I can't believe you just popped four babies out of you. Unreal."

"Kyle. I like Kyle," Amery said, looking at me.

"Yeah, I like Kyle, too," I said with a smile so wide it almost split my face in half.

"Thanks, I, um, like you guys, too," Kyle replied with a confused look.

"We meant for one of our sons." I snickered as I lifted our son who was in his hospital crib. "My mate was saying we should name our boy after you for getting me here in time for their birth."

"Really?" the vamp gasped as he glanced down at the sleeping bundle in my arms. I held my son out to him. "No way, I'd break him."

"You'll be fine," Amery said gently. "Just support his head."

"Okay," the cop whispered in awe as he took our son in his arms. "So you're really going to name this little guy Kyle?"

"If you'll let us," I said as I ran my fingers over my son's tiny hand.

"Yes please," Kyle replied quietly. "I've never had anyone named after me, and I've been alive almost as long as your mate. This is so cool."

"What about the other three?" my mom asked.

"Patrick?" I asked Amery after glancing at our son. We'd come up with four girls' names and four boys' names just so we had our bases covered. But staring down at the gorgeous creature in my mom's arms, I knew Patrick was the right choice.

"Yes, definitely," Amery said with a smile and tears in his eyes. Which of course started me and my mom all over again. And I even noticed that Officer Moran was trying to hide a few tears of his own. "And I think Aubrey and Leila for our girls."

I moved over and sat down on the side of his bed as I eyed our daughters over. I pointed to the one in his right arm first. "Yeah, she's totally an Aubrey." Then I gestured to our other girl. "And she's a Leila."

"I love you, babe," he whispered. I leaned over and brushed my lips to his. Did life get any better than this?

The nurse came in and announced that Amery and the babies needed to get some sleep now. Also that there were several policemen by the nurses' station looking for Officer Moran and me. So I gave my mate and each of my babies a kiss while Mom promised she'd watch over all of them while they slept.

Then I stepped out into the hall with Kyle and got the next part underway. It ended up we had to go down to the police station a few blocks away to get everything sorted out.

I got a few strange looks that I was smiling while explaining how I was kidnapped. But after I told them all I just became a daddy, they all understood. It seemed to take forever to give them my statement, and then I had to do a lineup to pick out Jake. The idiot went right back home after I escaped. Really, the guy needed to read some mysteries or watch some TV. He was the worst criminal ever! He so failed Evil Villain 101.

But once that was all done and Jake was in jail, Kyle took me back to the hospital. I smiled when he parked and came inside with me. It seemed our family made a new friend. He had a great time with my mom and playing with the babies while I lay in bed with Amery and cuddled.

"I can't believe we made those precious, tiny babies," I said with awe. "And I can't believe you were so strong and brave to bring them into the world. I wanted to faint just watching you."

"Really?" he asked with wide eyes. I turned my head and nodded so he could see. "But you are always so in control and know what to do."

"You're the medical guy." I chuckled. "You're like that when it comes to anyone's health. This is your domain."

"Thanks, my love," he whispered and then yawned. He drifted back to sleep, and everything was perfect. I held the man I loved in my arms, and our children were here and safe.

* * * *

The next week was a juggling act between four newborns, dealing with Jake and the police over the kidnapping, and the new construction on the clinic. Mom stayed, thankfully, or we might have drowned. One baby was a hard adjustment. Four was more than two men could handle.

We started calling agencies to find a full-time nanny, but for now Amery and I handled the daytime while Mom did the night. Sure, there was more during the day, but lots of times one of us got called away for this meeting or that. Plus, I still had writing to do for the magazine. Yeah, we needed help because my mom couldn't stay here forever.

It took us a couple of days to figure it out, but then we realized Kyle was a monkey, Aubrey was a witch, and Leila and Patrick were some combination of the two. Which I thought gave us a well-rounded family.

"Not sure we should have any more," Amery said as he collapsed into bed one night. "There's a spell I can place so I don't get pregnant again. It's the equivalent of a human getting her tubes tied."

"Let's wait until we're not completely exhausted parents of four newborns to decide," I replied with a yawn. "We don't want to do anything that can't be reversed."

"There's a counter spell if we change our minds later." He yawned loudly and didn't move even though he was still fully dressed.

"Then spell away, my love." I chuckled as I helped him get undressed. He muttered something unintelligible before falling deeply asleep.

I, on the other hand, opened up my laptop and just about fell over when I saw I had an email from Yolanda, Jake's wife. Oh, this couldn't be good.

*Amery & Kirby,*

*I wanted to write and apologize personally for what happened the day I came over. I truly thought that Amery stole the drugs to try and get Jake fired. I never had a clue that the man I married was so unhinged. And for the record, I am not infertile. We just haven't gotten pregnant yet. But after a few months of trying, he decreed I was and gave up trying. Now I understand that most of it had to do with him being in the closet and completely infatuated with Amery.*

*I was stupid enough to believe him when he said Amery came to him and begged Jake to take him back. I believed all of his lies until he said that the babies Amery was carrying were his. Then I started to realize that he'd had a mental breakdown.*

*I am sorry I caused you any distress, and I hope you will find it in your hearts to forgive me one day. I have no excuse or reason other than believing the man I loved and thought loved me.*

*Sincerely,*
*Yolanda*

Well, damn. I read it three times and forgave her. If Amery had told me the same shit Jake had spewed to her, I'd have jumped all over us, too. Maybe she was seeing what she wanted to see in Jake, or maybe he was better at hiding it until I came into the picture. I didn't know, and honestly I had so much good in my life I wasn't about to sit around and wonder about Jake's fucked-up mind.

He'd plead guilty to everything and was going to spend at least a good decade in jail for what he did in kidnapping me and stealing the drugs. The authorities also found a shitload of empty liquor bottles and anti-anxiety drugs at his home and office. It seemed this was a longtime problem of him denying his sexuality.

I did feel bad for Yolanda for one main reason. In his confession, he said that he always had planned to divorce her as soon as she gave him a few children and go back to Amery. She had cried when he'd said that, and Amery raced from the room to puke his guts out. I'd asked him about it later, and he swore up and down he would never have taken Jake back even if I hadn't come into the picture.

"That's just not something you do to someone you took vows with," Amery had said, shaking his head sadly. "If he loved me so much, we would have found a way to have children in his mind because he didn't know I was a witch. No matter what he says, I know in my heart he would never have come out of the closet."

"I'm glad he didn't and that left you single for us to meet," I replied as I helped him clean up. And I meant it. Meeting Amery after the Elders of UPAC tricked us was the best thing that had ever happened to me. Well, that and the birth of our children. Maybe they tied. And now that Jake was out of the picture, it was just our family and our love. It was all I ever wanted.

# Chapter 9

*Six months later*

"I'd like to welcome all of you to the grand opening of the United Paranormal Clinic of Colorado Springs," Amery said loudly into the microphone with a wide smile on his face. A roar of applause happened then, and I gave my mate up on the makeshift stage a wink.

Next to me, our twin nannies, Ginger and Cinnamon, whistled since they were each holding two babies and couldn't clap. They both had long blonde hair, but Ginger liked to keep hers shorter. And each personality was reflected in their beauty, but I tried not to grumble that they were taller than me.

Finding them was a blessing from the gods. They were two nineteen-year-old vampires who were thrown out of their close-minded coven because they wanted to go to college. Gag me. They had IQs off the charts and might be the most tender-hearted girls I'd ever met. They'd become more our family than our employees over the last five months.

When Elder Rice called to see if we could use them in the clinic, Amery had said to have them come interview. But after he interviewed them, he had me meet with them as well, and while I had no idea at the time what he was up to, I wanted to adopt them. Well, not literally since they were of age, but into our family nonetheless.

So we struck up a deal and had an addition put onto the house. They had their own apartment over the garage with a mini kitchen for basics, almost like a dorm room and everything. We paid for college, living expenses, books, food, and what not, and in return they had to keep a certain GPA with their classes and help us with the quadruplets.

Strange, I know, but it worked for us. And to top it off, they both wanted to be doctors one day in different fields. They even volunteered at the clinic on days when Amery and I took the kids out for a family day or on weekends when we were there to watch them. Now that the clinic was up and running starting tomorrow, they were going to continue to volunteer as candy stripers and with the e-book mobile I set up.

I had to admit that was one of my better ideas. I donated several Kindles with dozens upon dozens of books on them for all age levels so that everyone could always have something to read.

I'm not really sure when Ginger and Cinnamon slept, but they were young and loved the arrangement. And they loved our children, which was most important.

"I'm glad he went with the gray pin-stripe," Ginger whispered to me when the cheers died down. "He looks so powerful and commanding. Good call on that one. You so have to teach us your fashion sense."

"Does that mean you'll finally let me take you shopping?" I asked with a wink. Their coven had been very old-school and refused to use modern technology, not unlike the human Amish. But they had trouble breaking away from the long skirts and bland shirts. Hell, Ginger finally broke down and got her first pair of capris the other day.

I was wearing them down on their wardrobe.

"Fine, but no skirts shorter than mid thigh, and our cleavage stays in our shirts," Cinnamon said with an eye roll.

"Deal," I replied quickly before they changed their minds. I could work with that. It was the long-sleeve shirts all summer that drove me insane. I'd just look at them and feel myself sweating.

"There are so many people to thank for all their help and support," Amery said, and I focused back on the festivities. "All the Elders of

UPAC deserve a round of applause, but especially Elder Rice for getting the ball rolling and his constant advice. I'd also like to thank Shea Mayer for supplying all the state-of-the-art equipment we will all benefit from."

Both men on either side of my mate smiled and nodded at their acknowledgements. Shea's mates, Calin and Dustin, looked as if they were going to burst with pride. I had a suspicion I had the same look on my face.

It was such a small world at times. Calin and Dustin had both come from the same coven as Ginger and Cinnamon and knew them since they were babies, so they could attest to their character. That was a big reason we let them move in and helped them with college.

"I'd also like to thank my mate and the love of my life, Kirby Saxon," Amery said with emotion in his voice. "This would never have happened without him and his idea to help all paranormals receive the same care as humans without having to out themselves if they didn't want to. His constant support and willingness to do whatever was needed to make this clinic happen amazes and humbles me every day."

I felt the tears burn in my eyes but quickly blinked them away. Instead, I mouthed "I love you" to my man when everyone started clapping again. He mouthed it right back and then finished his speech when the applause died down. I felt almost giddy when he cut the ribbon and invited everyone to enter the clinic and have fun at the reception.

The clinic itself was gorgeous. It looked almost like a ritzy hotel instead of a medical facility. Since it was the first real paranormal medical facility, there was actually a hotel wing for out-of-town families of patients. It had reduced rates and facilitated to specific paranormal needs, like blood for vamps.

The architecture of the building was almost a work of art in itself. Somehow we'd gotten a world-renowned architect to design the place for an amount way under his normal fees since it was for a good cause. He'd also outed himself as a penguin shifter during the job and allowed *Sups Weekly* to do a spread on him. But from what I heard, he'd never been contacted for the amount of jobs and offers as he was now.

Guess his karma got a push for helping a nonprofit organization. But he seemed happy with it all.

Ginger, Cinnamon, still carrying the quadruplets, and I headed over to Amery as everyone else went inside to check out the facility. We got lots of stares when we went out in public. Two younger women pushing double strollers with just me or Amery as well got lots of attention.

"Great speech, honey," I said as he pulled me into his arms.

"I meant every word, babe," he whispered and then kissed me. I melted against him, wishing the reception was over. The kids were going home with Ginger and Cinnamon tonight, and we were staying at the attached hotel after the reception. Alone. Together. For the first time since they were born.

I had plans for tonight, and none of them involved clothes. But they did involve handcuffs and toys.

"Should they stay for a little while, or are we pushing nap time back too far?" I asked when we finally stopped locking lips.

"Half an hour? I kinda wanted to show it off to them now that they can be here and it's safe without construction materials all around." Amery looked at me with those puppy-dog eyes.

"They're six months old." I chuckled and waved the girls over to say they were staying for now. "I don't think they're going to remember this."

"I know, but they can feel the excitement around them, and that's always good for their brain stimulation," he said as his cheeks heated up. Fibber.

"I already waved them over." I loved my mate, and I also loved how far he'd come. Sure, he could still be timid at times and doubted his self-worth, but that was true of anyone. Gone were his constant worries that I'd leave and he couldn't be enough for me. It took us some work, but I knew we were stronger as a couple because of it.

"I love you," he said to me before leaning over the strollers. "And Daddy loves each of you very much. I hope when you get older and understand you'll be proud of what your dads did here today. We're trying to make sure you grow up in a better world."

Kyle made a monkey noise that warmed my heart. Don't get me wrong, I loved all of my children equally, I truly did. But I'd grown up around monkey-shifter babies and always dreamed of having one of my own one day. And when I heard my son make noises like that, it just made me realize I had everything I'd ever wished for and dreamed of.

We made our way inside and joined the fun. Everyone *oohed* and *aahed* over our babies, which of course filled our hearts with pride. Dustin and Calin were thrilled to see Ginger and Cinnamon, and I thought it was good for them to see someone from their coven who had survived leaving like they did. And they were ridiculously happy with their mate, so I thought that gave them hope that they would have that one day, too.

Amery and I made the rounds, and he introduced me to most of the new staff whose names I wouldn't remember. I was pretty sure of that after how many I met in one night. But I was going to try since my mate was the man in charge and our nannies were volunteering there. Plus, everyone was just so nice and excited to be a part of the clinic that I truly saw us all making our own extended family or pack of paranormals.

Not that any more paranormals I wasn't sleeping with were going to be moving into our home.

The party rocked. The music was perfect, the food was delicious, the company was great, and everyone was smiling and having fun. Even the humans that were there didn't seem to even be fazed that they were the minority there. Hell, the mayor of Colorado Springs was chatting up a pretty werewolf doctor most of the night. It gave me hope, to say the least, that paranormals would be accepted everywhere one day.

But for now, the kids had long gone home with Ginger and Cinnamon. The reception was over, and we'd said good-bye to all of our guests like good hosts. The out-of-town ones checked into the hotel, and I'd not heard about any complaints, which thrilled me. All the locals had left, mostly in cabs after the amount of alcohol we'd all consumed and with smiles on their faces.

And I was in our room with my mate...alone. We were both happy, tipsy from the champagne, and ready for what came next. Without a word, I led Amery over to the bed, which I'd snuck into the room earlier to set up. His eyes went wide and his mouth hung open at everything I had laid out on the king-size bed.

"Are you ready to be my personal sex slave tonight, my mate?" I asked with a purr as I loosened his tie.

"Yes, my love," he said in a shaky voice.

"You can top me if you want, honey." I wasn't sure if he was apprehensive of giving complete control to me or just excited. He didn't hesitate in answering as I worked on his shirt next.

"No! I want everything you have planned for me."

"Then get naked in the next minute or I'm ripping your clothes off," I said firmly with a growl. He licked his lips and nodded as he got to work. I lost my clothes just as quickly, and soon we were next to the bed naked.

"Can I kiss you?"

"Always," I whispered as I leaned forward and planted my hands on his chest as I stood on my toes. His lips brushed mine a few times before I claimed his lips as I planned on doing his body. All. Night. Long.

"I'm ready to blow already, Kirby," he whimpered against my lips. "Can we take the edge off first?"

"Already way ahead of you. Get on the bed and put your hands over your head."

He shivered at the commanding tone in my voice and climbed onto the bed. I followed right behind him and locked the handcuffs around each wrist and looped it through the headboard. I pulled on them gently to make sure they were really on there and was pleased they would hold him unless he went nuts.

Which really wasn't a bad thing if he did in my book.

I made a big show of starting with his lips and kissing down his body as I reached out and picked up what I had planned for round one. His eyes went wide and he started to pant when I put the finger vibrator on and poured some lube on it. Then I rubbed it over his tight hole as I licked the head of his dripping cock.

We'd been so busy with the opening that we went a whole three days doing no more than just kissing. We were too newly mated for that to be acceptable, and I planned on making that up and more tonight.

"Start slow or fast?" I asked him to see if he was on the edge as much as I was.

"Fast! Hard! Shove it in," he gasped as his hips started to move. I did as he asked, pushing it into his ass and rubbing it against his sweet spot. All it took was two more licks of my tongue and he cried out my name and shot reams of seed all over his body.

"Good boy," I cooed as he started to come back down. I hadn't removed the vibrator and used it to open him up for me as his orgasm rocked his body.

"Oh fuck, I think I'm going to come again," he moaned and pulled at the handcuffs. "I love you, Kirby."

"Love you, too," I replied as I quickly pulled the toy out, shut it off, and used the excess lube to slick up my cock. "Lift your hips."

He nodded and did what I wanted so I could push a couple of pillows under his ass. "Am I allowed to talk?"

"Anything you want, honey." I chuckled. Did he think I was going to be his Dom tonight and make him call me sir? It seemed he almost wanted that. Something to think about for a later time.

"Pound that big cock in my ass," he begged. I smiled wickedly at him and spread his legs wider. He loved feeling as if we were doing acrobatics during sex and pushing the limits. I slammed my dick into him, bottoming out in one shot. We both moaned at the overload of pleasant sensations racking our body.

"I'm not going to last long," I panted as I pulled back out until just the head of my cock was left in him. He nodded, and I thrust back in with everything I had. Nothing was more erotic than the sight of my mate squirming around on the bed in the throes of passion from what I was doing to him. Amery made the sexiest noises and whimpers that egged me on until I was fucking him so hard and fast I felt like I was running a marathon.

"Fill me, babe," he moaned as I pecked that special spot again. That was all it took. My body was practically seizing from the force of my climax.

"Amery!" I screamed at the top of my lungs as my dick exploded and shot deep, deep inside of him. Holy shit! Maybe waiting a few days in between sex might be worth it if we had orgasms like this.

Then again, maybe not.

He followed me right over, cried out in pleasure as he shot all over us. My monkey was thrilled that our mate was covering us in his seed, his scent, and his very essence. I kept pushing in and out of him until I didn't have a drop left in me and Amery was spent as well. And then I collapsed like a sack of potatoes on top of him.

"Love you, my mate, my heart, my soul," I said in between gasps for air as I pulled out of him and then kissed up his body.

"Me, too, Kirby," he whispered as I kissed him deeply. I reached over us and released his hands. The second I did, he wrapped them around me and rolled us over. "Please say I get to claim you next? Was that in the plan?"

"Absolutely," I answered with a wink as I reached over for the next toy. I held up a big purple vibrator for him to see, wiggling it in my hand. "After you fuck me with this and make me blow."

"My pleasure," he replied in that deep, sexy voice of his that always made me shiver. He grabbed it from me and took over our fun with a big smile on his face the whole time. I'm sure I had one on my face as well as he rocked my world.

I never thought in a million years that something as simple as the UPAC conference and the turn of events there would have me six months later with four children, two nannies that were almost family, and the most wonderful, perfect mate for me. And more than I needed in life, it was everything I'd ever wanted, and I'd never, ever regret deciding to attend that year's conference. Damn, I really did need to send the Elders that fruit basket now.

# THE END

**WWW.JOYEEFLYNN.COM**

# ABOUT THE AUTHOR

Joyee Flynn grew up in Chicago living in the same house all her life until she left for college. Though she has a great life, she loves to get lost in fantasy that only books could bring. Her wide interest in reading was reflected in her writings. Currently Joyee lives with her dog, Marius, named after a vampire from Ann Rice's Interview with the Vampire series. She dreams of one day living out in Montana, enough land to have a few horses, and find a couple of cowboys of her own.

A lover of men, Joyee's all about them in any form in her books. Vampire, werewolf, military, doesn't matter at all as long as they are hot, hard, and sex fiends!

## *Also by Joyee Flynn*

Siren Classic ManLove: Midnight Matings: *Squeak and a Roar*
Siren Classic ManLove: Midnight Matings: *Two Fangs and a Hoof*
Siren Classic ManLove: Midnight Matings: *Fur and Flightless*

*For all other titles, please visit*
www.bookstrand.com/joyee-flynn

**Siren Publishing, Inc.**
**www.SirenPublishing.com**

Lightning Source UK Ltd.
Milton Keynes UK
UKOW031502291011

181148UK00002B/16/P